Two hands came out to grasp her shoulders

Alex pulled her close to the lean, powerful length of his body, his taunting mouth only a whisper away as he said, "Stay away from my father. I've met your sort before and I won't have him hurt. And if you think I'm the underdog around here, all bark and no bite, forget it."

"So you're the power behind the throne now, are you?" Imogen could match his derision, breath for breath, if it suited her.

"I prefer the title of troubleshooter, as far as you're concerned." His hard fingers tightened, biting into her flesh, and his mouth curled sardonically. "So show some sense, lady, and don't tangle with me."

DIANA HAMILTON creates high-tension conflict that brings new life to traditional romance. Readers find her a welcome addition to Harlequin and look forward to new novels by this talented author.

Books by Diana Hamilton

DIANA HAMILTON

Troubleshooter

Harlequin Books

TORONTO • NEW YORK • LONDON
AMSTERDAM • PARIS • SYDNEY • HAMBURG
STOCKHOLM • ATHENS • TOKYO • MILAN
MADRID • WARSAW • BUDAPEST • AUCKLAND

Harlequin Presents first edition June 1993
ISBN 0-373-11563-6

Original hardcover edition published in 1992
by Mills & Boon Limited

TROUBLESHOOTER

CHAPTER ONE

IMOGEN stretched luxuriously beneath the light duvet and lazily swept the heavy mass of her pale ash-blonde hair away from her face with both hands. It was bliss to be able to come awake slowly, her normal morning scramble to get ready for work a thing of the past for the next three weeks.

Her deep-violet eyes came fully awake first, focusing on the dainty furnishings of her small, uncluttered bedroom, the first rays of the early autumn sun filtering through the pale apple-green curtains.

A faint frown-line pulled her arching brows together. The coming three weeks of her annual leave entitlement should give her ample time to decide whether or not to accept Tolly's job offer and shake the dust of the Martin and Sandown advertising agency off her feet.

But she was not going to think about that now, she decided with her customary incisiveness. For the next few days she was determined to relax, allow her disillusionment over the way she had been treated by the agency to settle, letting her see the wood for the trees. Stupid to walk out of a job she was good at, could handle with one hand tied behind her back, in a moment of pique.

She slid out of bed and reached for her robe, tying the belt round her small waist, the silky fabric clinging to her high round breasts, floating around her endless legs as she walked through to the kitchen to make herself coffee.

Collecting the morning papers from the box outside her doorway in the hall of the apartment block, she added them to her tray and carried it back to bed. She was meeting Tolly for lunch but until then she had nothing to do but laze around, pamper herself.

She was smiling as she settled back against the pillows, the coffee-tray on the bedside table, the morning papers on her knees, and her smile deepened as her eyes scanned the news items, fastening on the photograph of herself and Tolly leaving his exclusive London hotel.

The photo-journalist had caught them at what would appear to be an intimate moment, she smiling up into his eyes, a trick of the light making her expression look almost stupidly adoring, his arm around her shoulder determinedly possessive. And the guy had gone to town on the text.

She read through it quickly, a ripple of inner laughter making her eyes sparkle.

Millionaire store owner Anatol Khristoforo Devenko, sixty-nine, making a rare appearance in Britain. Does the length of his stay have anything to do with the elegant Imogen Paige, twenty-five, his close companion for the last few weeks? When questioned, Miss Paige replied coyly, 'We are just good friends.' No doubt the beautiful Imogen feels that the size of his bank balance closes the age-gap very adequately.

It was too absurd to be taken seriously. No one who knew her would believe the gold-digger label and Tolly would throw back his still-handsome head and roar with laughter when he read the trashy piece. So far as she could tell the only thing he ever took seriously was his business, the world-wide chain of outrageously up-market stores. It was said that you could find anything in Devenko's, provided it was beautiful, exclusive and expensive.

The Devenko chain offered a completely new shopping experience with superb-quality goods from all over the world, classy restaurants, health and beauty salons, all under the same roof. A quick shaft of half-fearful excitement flicked around in her stomach. The Devenko name was deservedly world famous and Tolly had singled her out, offering her the job of running the advertising and promotion campaigns for the entire chain, the pay and working conditions something not even her most ambitious dreams had ever contemplated. It would be a huge responsibility and taking it on board was something she had to think very seriously about.

'As always, you look fascinatingly lovely.' Tolly's brown eyes were amused as the waiter moved out of earshot, his mouth a twitch away from laughter as he looked at her over the table in the quiet, discreetly luxurious restaurant he favoured. 'The suit is new, yes? It is perfect, you are perfect. Playing up to the wicked Press?'

'You read it?' No need to ask, his sudden grin told her he had. 'Pitiful, wasn't it?' she smiled, watching as he took a sip of his sherry and rolled it appreciatively around his tongue.

He was very astute; she had made a special effort this morning, sweeping her heavy, silky hair high on her head to emphasise the elegant length of her neck, the classical purity of her features, her suit a structured, extravagantly expensive piece of power-dressing in a muted amethyst that made her eyes look like bruised pansies against the creamy whiteness of her skin.

'Maybe.' He took up her comment. 'But flattering also, for me. That anyone should couple my name romantically with that of a beautiful, highly intelligent woman is enough to make a man of my age puff up with pride just a little.'

Imogen shook her head at him, her smile wry. At sixty-nine Tolly was still an attractive man, his iron-grey hair neatly groomed and thick, his figure upright and, as always, expensively clad.

'Don't sell yourself short,' she told him, beginning on her first course of Waldorf salad. 'The piece implied you were having to buy me. I imagine it will be a long time before you have to use bribes to get a woman to be part of your life.'

Although she felt she had got to know him well over the past few weeks Imogen knew next to nothing about his private life, except that he had a son, at present visiting the European branches of the stores. Alexsander, she had been told, was thirty-six, at present the financial director of the chain, would one day take his father's place as chairman, was engaged to his second cousin... It was all she knew, and all she wanted to know.

She was a private person herself, keeping her emotions locked up inside her head. Her earlier memories of her parents' fights, loud voices, banged doors, long periods of brooding, hateful silences had put them there. And now her parents were divorced, both remarried and settled abroad, her mother in Greece, her father in New Zealand, and Imogen got on with her life, her career, keeping herself to herself.

'And that I do regret.' Tolly wasn't smiling now. 'For you the insinuations must have been particularly galling.' He lowered his voice. 'I can only admire you for taking it so well and thank you for not telling the truth.'

The truth. That Anatol Devenko was in London to negotiate the purchase of a failing department store which, because of its prime site, was arousing serious interest in property developing circles. If it became known that Tolly intended to buy out the store, create Devenko's London, then the competition would go into top gear. Only he, his son and his financial advisers knew of his interest. And Imogen, of course.

She said, 'I keep my promises,' wrinkling her nose at him, making him smile again.

He assured her, 'You won't have to hold your tongue much longer. By early evening I should know if my offer has been accepted. Going by my last meeting with the vendors' management, I have every confidence that it will be. And that will bring us to another turning in our relationship.'

He leaned back as one waiter removed the debris of their first course and another presented the second, and Imogen thought, The job offer, of course! and the familiar swirl of excited panic set up inside her again.

'Yes, I know,' she said inadequately. She had banked on having more time to reach a decision. And he must have seen the indecision on her face because he said drily,

'Don't panic. You can give me your answer later; ten more minutes won't hurt either of us. In the meantime, eat.'

So she did, barely tasting the delicious food, her mind whirling backwards over the past few weeks.

She had first met Tolly at the promotional thrash given by Martin and Sandown for the launch of the new 'Jewels' range. For eighteen months she had worked almost exclusively on the 'Jewels' young fashion account, and when her boss, the account executive with overall control of the campaign, had taken early retirement, she had confidently expected to step into his shoes because she alone, during the past twelve months when his health had been failing, had taken virtually sole responsibility for the promotions and full responsibility for the launch of the products from the linked 'Jewels' range of personal toiletries.

She had been so confident, that the news that a newcomer had been brought in over her head—male, needless to say—had come like a body-blow, sending her reeling. The firm's directors, almost to a man, were decidedly chauvinistic. She had always known that but had thought that she had proved her worth to the extent that her sex would not be held against her.

How wrong she had been. But she had gone through her paces at the party, not allowing her feelings to show. It was something she had become good at since her miserable, sometimes frightening experiences in childhood had taught her self-reliance, the need never to show anyone how much she was hurting inside.

The invitation, through one of his secretaries, to have dinner with Anatol Devenko at his hotel to discuss a business proposition, had come the following day. She remembered him clearly from the evening before, and had been intrigued.

She was used to men who made passes and could handle them, but would prefer not to have to if she could avoid it. But she prided herself on being an astute judge of character and didn't believe, for one moment, that Devenko was about to make one.

He didn't. He offered her a job, told her quite frankly that he was head-hunting, had noted her success with the 'Jewels' account and wanted her to handle the advertising promotions for the entire Devenko's chain.

At the moment agencies in the base countries handled the accounts separately, but the result, he felt, was bitty, uncoordinated. He needed the umbrella of his own agency, and he wanted her to head it. She would have an excellent back-up team, the services of translators, complete control and a salary that took her breath away when he quoted it.

So why was she hesitating? She had climbed as far up the ladder at Martin and Sandown as she was ever likely to go—recent events had spelt that out in letters a mile high. She wasn't afraid of responsibility and knew she was good at her job. And she liked Tolly, admired and respected him, so working for him wouldn't cause any problems.

Over the past weeks she had got to know him well, accepting his invitations to dine, to take in a show, even, on several weekends, showing him the tourist spots, never once letting on to anyone that a job with him was in the offing because, as far as anyone else was allowed to know, Anatol Devenko was in London as a sightseer, and if their names had become linked and people saw them as an item it didn't really matter.

There must be a strong puritanical streak in her somewhere, she decided, absently sipping her wine. Deep down she felt that success had to be earned. Everything she had achieved had been by her own hard work; her parents had been too busy snapping and snarling at each other, throwing objects as well as tantrums, to take any notice of their quiet, introspective child, let alone help her in her choice of career.

And Tolly's job offer went way beyond her wildest dreams. It had been handed to her on a plate, she felt, and didn't quite trust the idea of instant and enormous success.

'Perhaps I might suggest something that could take your mind off the obviously intimidating prospect of working for me.' Tolly broke into her thoughts with a wry smile that made her want to deny that he, personally, had anything to do with her hesitation. 'I would like your opinion, as a sophisticated and extremely talented young woman, on a house I am thinking of buying.'

'A house?' Imogen echoed, immediately distracted. Tolly, so he had told her, had been born in the States, had lived there all his life. At the age of almost seventy she couldn't imagine him disrupting himself to that extent. 'Here? In London? You mean you want to live here?'

He dipped his iron-grey head. 'Just outside Windsor. I would like to be based here while my new store is being created. I am not so young that I relish the thought of flying the Atlantic at regular intervals, and not yet quite so old that I could contemplate living in a hotel for what could be an extensive period of time. Also, there is the setting up of our own agency, here in London. I would like to be on hand to offer you my advice, should you require it.' His brown eyes twinkled warmly, as if her acceptance of the job were a foregone conclusion. He refilled her wine glass. 'Also, my son will need a settled home when he marries. At the moment he tends to live out of suitcases, and, as the company's business brings him often to Europe, a house near London would be ideal for him and Catrina.'

'Then perhaps your son and his fiancée should be the ones to vet it, not I,' Imogen suggested drily, privately thinking that Tolly's son and heir sounded a wimp if, at the age of thirty-six, he hadn't the gumption to find himself a settled home. Being the only child of an extremely wealthy father, he was probably used to having everything done for him and was unable to do anything for himself.

'But I don't know when Alex will be back from Europe,' Tolly told her softly. 'And Catrina is with friends somewhere in the Bahamas, so it is up to me. Besides, buying a house here was my idea. The two young people know nothing about it.' He finished his wine off and set the glass down with a click. 'If I present them with a ready-made home it might make them decide to name the day. One can always hope. Coffee, my dear?'

She nodded and said, 'I'd love some.' Presumably, the unknown Catrina was holding back. Imogen didn't blame her. Alexsander Devenko sounded a wash-out. 'Then the date of the wedding hasn't been set?' she asked, not really interested but simply finding something to say to delay the moment when she would have to either commit herself to taking the job he offered or cry off.

'Unhappily, no.' He spread his hands. 'Catrina would have him tomorrow, but Alex is difficult to pin down. Eventually, of course, they will marry; they are very much in love. It is what I hoped for from the moment she was born. Alex, of course, was only twelve years old at the time, but 'Stasia, Catrina's mother, was my cousin—we put our heads together later and planned a union between our offspring. Not only would such a marriage hold the family together, it would consolidate the business. Catrina, through her mother, inherits a sizeable holding of Devenko's shares.'

Imogen had heard of dynastic marriages before and Tolly's history was common knowledge. His father had been born in the Ukraine and become an officer in the Imperial White Russian army. He had arrived in the States in 1920 as a refugee, with his wife, and Tolly had been born six months later. It had been his father who had started the first innovative and exclusive store, using borrowed capital and, somewhere along the line, his aunt and his young cousin Anastasia had arrived, fleeing from the revolution. Then, years later, Anastasia had married an American who had put money into Devenko's, and thus a financial dynasty had been born.

It was little wonder Tolly had set his heart on the marriage, but Imogen thought he was deluding himself if he imagined the couple were in love. Simple arithmetic informed her that Catrina would be twenty-four now; had it been a love match they could have married four or five years ago.

'There will be a chauffeur-driven car waiting outside in roughly half an hour,' Tolly told her. 'And I would be more than grateful if you would come with me to view the property.'

'Put like that, how could I refuse?' Imogen smiled softly, never ceasing to be impressed by his old-fashioned courtesy, and he put his hand over hers, his eyes warm.

'Thank you, my dear. As always, I am honoured to have the privilege of your company.'

And somewhere behind them, in a voice that would have frozen a lava flow, someone said, 'Is this a private party, or can anyone join in?'

'Alex!' After a moment of stunned surprise, Tolly sprang to his feet with an agility that made a mockery of his years, clamping his hands on the younger, much taller man's shoulders, affection radiating from his warm brown eyes. And Imogen felt her breath catch in her throat.

Words like 'wimp' and 'wash-out' flew straight out of her head. Alexsander Devenko was very definitely a man who knew what he wanted and knew how to get it. Success and achievement were written all over him, from the authoritative carriage of his dark head and broad shoulders to the soles of his hand-made shoes.

'When did you arrive in England?' Tolly was asking. 'Why didn't you let me know?' Imogen had never seen him look so happy before; he was like a dog with a tail which couldn't stop wagging.

Alex said drily, 'It was a spur-of-the-moment decision. I flew in from Paris by executive jet this morning.' His voice was dark, like rough velvet, and, unaccountably, Imogen felt her spine tingle as he continued, 'As soon as I touched down I contacted your hotel. One of your army of secretaries told me you were lunching here. I came straight away.'

It was a voice she could listen to forever, but Tolly cut in, 'It's so good to see you, my boy. And you'll join us for coffee, of course, and——' He turned, looking mortified. 'My dear, what must you think of me? Imogen, allow me, belatedly, to introduce my son, Alexsander. Alex, this is my very good friend, Imogen Paige.'

She could see that the lapse in his normally impeccable manners worried him, and she gave him a soft, sympathetic smile before turning her attention to the younger man.

And then her smile died as she met his narrowed, contemptuous gaze and saw the hard, compressed line of his mouth.

'Miss Paige,' he acknowledged unsmilingly, subjecting her to a long, offensive stare from cold amber eyes, and Imogen frowned, not used to meeting such open animosity. But Tolly, it seemed, had noticed nothing amiss, had organised fresh coffee, an extra cup, and he said,

'Spend the afternoon with us. Imogen and I are on our way to look at a house in Windsor I'm thinking of buying. I'd value your opinion, too.' He smiled expansively, no doubt thinking of the day when he'd be able to hand it over to the engaged couple.

Imogen saw the younger man's face ice over, his mouth tightening as he stated, 'I wouldn't miss it for a king's ransom,' his eyes narrowing as his father nodded his approval, excused himself and left for the wash-room, Alex's voice spitting tacks as he added, 'He's not safe to be let out on his own.'

Imogen sucked in her breath, her spine rigid. In a matter of minutes her opinion of Alexsander Devenko had turned a few somersaults. The wimp of her imaginings had been transformed into a definitely masculine, highly attractive achiever. But that impression had only lasted seconds. Right now she was looking at an arrogant, cold-hearted, boorish bastard, and she said snappily,

'Your father happens to be one of the most capable men I know, and that makes your remark uncalled for. Doubly so, since he also possesses both charm and good manners, neither of which you would apparently understand if they were spelled out to you in words of one tiny syllable!'

She could feel the flush of unaccustomed rage burn across her ivory skin, obliterating her normal cool sophistication. But for some reason she didn't care that for once she was allowing her emotions to master her common sense. He had no right to sit there, his brooding amber eyes staring right through her, talking as though his father were senile.

And he drawled, 'I'm sure he'd be flattered by your testimonial.' He leaned back in his seat, his aggressively handsome features stony, the immaculately tailored three-piece suit he wore evidence of perfect taste and the financial clout to express it. 'But then, there's no fool like an old fool, is there? However, I happen to be extremely fond of my father and I'm not prepared to sit quietly on the sidelines and watch some little gold-digger make a monkey out of him.'

Imogen stared at him, her eyes going very wide, like pools of ink, her full lips dropping open. For a moment she was in shock. She simply couldn't believe she was hearing this.

Then the adrenalin began to flow, pumping through her veins, and she pulled herself together, got to her feet.

'I'm not staying here to listen to any more of this garbage!' she snapped. 'Perhaps you'd explain to your father why I prefer to wait for him outside.'

Let him get out of that! she thought, fuming. But he caught her wrist, pulling her back down again.

'You can leave when I tell you to. And then, lady, it had better be for good. Whenever I'm abroad I buy the English papers. As soon as I read that piece about you and my father being "just good friends" I came over to put a stop to it. So, as I said, when you go, you go for good.'

Imogen drew in a deep, painful breath. Her pulses were pounding a quick-fire tattoo and any minute now she would forget she had ever known how to hide her emotions and create a scene people would remember for years to come!

But she was saved from such an indignity by Tolly's return to the table, and quickly, and with some difficulty, schooled her features to blankness. If she repeated his son's disgusting accusations he would be understandably hurt, and she didn't want that. So she had to grit her teeth and hold on to her temper when Alex stood up and turned to his father.

'Let me have the address of the house. I'll meet up with you there later. And don't leave the place before I get there. There's no way I'm letting you buy a pig in a poke.' And, although he smiled for his father, his eyes, when they met hers, were very cold, the ambiguity of his remark not lost on her as he nodded briefly in her direction.

'I'm sure we'll meet later, Miss Paige. Believe me, I'm looking forward to it.'

CHAPTER TWO

THE chauffeur-driven limo drew up to the kerb in Sloane Street as Imogen and Tolly left the restaurant, and she slid into the pampered luxury of the rear seat beside the elderly man and wanted to say 'Is your son always so objectionable?' but didn't, of course.

She deeply regretted her promise to accompany Tolly this afternoon but, short of telling him she couldn't bear the idea of meeting up with his over-bearingly arrogant and self-opinionated son again, there was nothing she could do.

Alexsander Devenko had looked at her as if she were dirt and no one, no one, had ever done that to her before. And how dared he accuse her of being a common little gold-digger? How dared he?

Thankfully, Tolly was engrossed in an expensively produced package of estate agent's particulars, so failed to pick up the simmering rage that held her speechless and fuming. He was gloating over colour photographs, reading out loud.

'Seven bedrooms, three en suite, two separate bathrooms, four reception, study, large kitchen, utility quarters, garden room—and a range of out-buildings, too. See, Imogen——' He passed the bundle over to her, stabbing a forefinger at where he wanted her to look. 'Stabling, too, a paddock and two acres of carefully tended gardens. For a family home, it couldn't be better.'

Imogen looked at the expected price and echoed hollowly, 'Couldn't be better.' And it couldn't—not if one was the sort who looked on a million-plus as loose change!

Years ago, before she'd met the charming, un-assuming man who was now poring over his particulars again, she'd read an article that had named Anatol Khristoforo Devenko, chairman and major shareholder in Devenko's, as one of America's richest men, a self-made man with the Midas touch! And he'd need to be if he could consider buying such a property in the sole hope of tempting his son and future daughter-in-law to settle down to married life and the raising of sons who would carry the dynasty well on into the twenty-first century.

'Also a large service flat over the stable block,' Tolly was intoning, as if he couldn't believe his good fortune. 'Ideal for a housekeeper and gardener; Catrina, bless her, is not exactly a home-body, and the nanny could always live in, of course.'

He was jumping the gun, Imogen thought, re-laxing back against the leather upholstery. Tolly obviously thought his wretched son was the best thing since the Creation and had credited the absent Catrina with a willingness to tie herself down to the hand-picked boor that wasn't there.

If she had been pressured into becoming engaged to Alexsander Devenko, then she, too, would have taken herself off to some remote Bahamian retreat for the duration!

She couldn't voice her thoughts; for one thing she didn't know Tolly well enough and, for another, she wouldn't dream of spoiling the elderly man's rosy dreams—so she gazed out of the window and kept her cynical doubts to herself.

Although the traffic out of London had seemed heavy, the big, expertly driven car had made Windsor in an hour, and there, on the skyline, was the familiar but never-taken-for-granted sight of the oldest inhabited castle in the world, dominating the attractive town in spirit and in fact.

The streets with their Victorian, Georgian and even older buildings were still, late in the season, thronged with tourists intent on visiting the precincts of the chief royal residence. Originally built by William the Conqueror, the castle had been added to by practically every sovereign since, and now covered thirteen acres; and Imogen wished she were one of the tourists, just wandering idly around the town, perhaps looking for one of the tea-shops where she could rest her feet. Anywhere but where she was, destined at some time in the not too distant future to cross swords with one of the nastiest people she had ever met!

Ten minutes later they were drawing up in front of one of the loveliest Queen Anne houses Imogen had ever seen, and almost before the car had stopped Tolly was out, hurrying round to hand her out as if she were a princess, taking her arm as he guided her to where the agent was waiting, apparently by appointment, to show them round.

'I can't wait!' Tolly said, rubbing his hands, looking so like a little boy with a stack of birthday presents to be opened that Imogen wanted to hug him. For all his business brain, success and money, he was one of the nicest, most uncomplicated people she had ever met. She couldn't imagine how he had sired such an objectionable son!

As soon as she decently could, Imogen excused herself and wandered outside. The house was undeniably beautiful and in excellent repair but she wasn't particularly interested in seeing where Alex would live with his bride. Or so Tolly hoped!

She felt deeply sorry for the unknown Catrina, doubtlessly pressured into agreeing to marry for dynastic reasons, she thought, gently closing the elegant main door behind her and breathing deeply of the crisp, bright autumn air.

The gardens were superb and overlooked Windsor Great Park—two thousand acres of beautifully wooded land—and no one would ever believe that the sprawling, teeming suburbs of the capital were so close.

For something to pass the time Imogen made her way to the outbuildings just glimpsed between graceful stands of trees, their leaves beginning to turn colour, and realised her mistake when she drew nearer and saw the silver glint of the sleek Jaguar pulled up on the paved forecourt.

That man! That odious man!

She turned to go, but not quickly enough because that deep, sexy voice, an edge of steel in it now, bit out,

'Not so fast. I want a word with you.'

She wouldn't be seen to run. Certainly not by him. And so she faced him, the classical sophistication of her features schooled to indifference.

He was emerging from one of the large outbuildings and he walked towards her, his hard mouth straight, his dark golden eyes moving over her elegant, expensively clad body in a cold, assessing stare. And, to her annoyance, Imogen felt the beginnings of a flush begin to spread across her high, wide cheekbones. It wasn't pleasant to be on the receiving end of such grim dislike.

'Been looking around, have you? Poking your nose into your father's business again?'

If this was to be war, and he had made that much clear earlier on, then she was going to fire the first shots, and the glint of anger in his eyes told her she'd been right on target. And that certainly made the adrenalin flow, she acknowledged inside her head as she lifted one darkly arched brow in cool disdain and felt her heart begin to pump like a mad thing.

She hoped to heaven that she looked cooler and braver than she felt. A couple of hours earlier he had thrown down the gauntlet and she wasn't the sort to look away and pretend she hadn't noticed.

'My father is not a young man. I make his business my business.' He was close now, her eyes were on the level of his firm, aggressive chin and she could feel his distaste for her coming off him in waves.

His dark head was tilted slightly to one side and he was rocking back on his heels, his long legs apart, his hands thrust negligently into the pockets of his trousers, his jacket open, showing the waistcoat that clipped his lean waist. And he looked dangerous, sounded even more so when he told her silkily, 'My father may be front-runner for the company, the figure-head, but never forget for one moment that I'm right there behind him, calling the shots. If he wants to buy a house, or a woman, I make it my business to know about it.'

'And stop it? Jealous, are you?' she countered icily, hiding the swift run of rage as best she could. It would be fatal to let him know he could make her lose her temper. She had already lost her temper and dignity, back in the restaurant, and she hated the loss of control. She never let her emotions show if she could help it.

'Jealous?' Alex came back with unhidden derision. 'Of you? I don't fancy women who can be bought. You never know where they have been.'

The calculated insult took her breath away, made hot colour burn in her face, and her eyes were more black than violet as she dragged in a breath through pinched nostrils and turned to stalk away. But two hard hands came out to grasp her shoulders, hauling her close to the lean, powerful length of his body, his taunting mouth only a whisper away as he said,

'Stay away from him. I've met your sort before and I won't have him hurt. And if you think I'm the underdog around here, all bark and no teeth, forget it. As I said before, I call the shots.'

'So you're the power behind the throne now, are you?' Imogen could match his derision, breath for breath, if it suited her. And she stood very still beneath his hands because to struggle would be futile.

He was far stronger than she, and she wouldn't give him the satisfaction of subduing her physically.

'I prefer the title of troubleshooter as far as you're concerned.' His hard fingers tightened, biting into her flesh, and his mouth curled sardonically. 'So show some sense, lady, and don't tangle with me. I want you out of my father's life, as of now.'

She met his hard golden stare head on, her own eyes cold with fury. What right had he to sit in judgement on her? To call her names on the strength of a silly piece in a mindless gossip column?

About to tell him as much, her voice died in her throat as she heard Tolly call her name, his footsteps sounding near as he walked through the trees. Alex released her, stepping back as if from contaminated material, his hard, handsome face tight with dislike as he bit out,

'Do as I say, or I'll personally break you,' and swung away to meet his father, leaving Imogen to stare after him with angry eyes, at his lithe, perfectly proportioned male body taut with arrogance.

Hateful bastard! How dared he threaten her, assume the worst without stopping to ask questions, listen to answers? Her heart was pumping erratically, her breath coming in shallow gasps. She could follow him now, through the trees, confront the two men together, demand that Tolly tell his loathsome offspring the exact nature of their relationship.

But she wouldn't, she knew she wouldn't.

No way would she put her case to that arrogant devil, make a plea for a fair trial, show anxiety to have her innocence proved.

She'd see him in hell first!

She did join them, of course she did. But she was very cool now, her emotions perfectly controlled, and the glint of almost malicious devilment deep in her amethyst eyes was carefully veiled by the sultry sweep of thick, dark lashes.

The two men were deep in conversation but Tolly's eyes lit up when he saw her. 'So there you are. I thought I'd lost you!'

Smiling softly, she tucked her arm through his. 'You knew I wouldn't be far away.' And the huskiness of her voice was no act at all because the look of stony distaste she'd received from Alex Devenko had pushed her breath back into her lungs.

Far from looking surprised by her unprecedented physical gesture, Tolly had beamed with pleasure, patting her hand as it lay on his arm. And he would have taken her statement at face value. But Alex hadn't. He was adept at reading things that weren't there.

'I was just telling Alex that, apart from my using this house—should I decide to buy—as a base while we create Devenko's London, I would deed it to him and Catrina, when they marry.'

He turned back to his stony-faced son and Imogen thought, I bet that knocked some of the wind out of your sails. You thought he was buying it to share with me.

And Tolly, sublimely unaware of the undercurrents, suggested, 'So you'd better look around. The agent had to leave. I'll return the key on the way back.'

Tolly, of course, had to accompany his son, pointing out the obvious perfections of the house, and Imogen would have opted to walk in the gardens if it hadn't been for the overwhelmingly powerful need to show Alexsander High-and-Mighty Devenko that he couldn't threaten her!

He would soon discover that his assumptions about her relationship with his father were way off-mark but, until he did, let him stew. She would do everything she could to show him that no way would she take any notice at all of his stinging threats. Let him think she was here to stay, clinging on to his father's arm, making herself very available in return for the goodies a man of Tolly's wealth could offer. She hoped his blood-pressure went through the roof!

So she stuck like a limpet to Tolly's side. He had invited her along, after all, and he wasn't to know that her act of hanging on his every utterance, smiling until her face felt stiff, was anything other than friendly interest.

But Alex knew differently, or thought he did. And, although he pointedly ignored her, treated her comments as unspoken, she knew she was getting right under his skin by the way a muscle jerked spasmodically at the side of his jaw, his shoulders rigid with temper as he ran lightly down the stairs ahead of them.

'Well, what do you think?' Tolly asked as Alex locked the main door behind them and handed the keys back to his father.

'The house can't be faulted,' he stated, his dark velvet voice sending annoying trickles of sensation down Imogen's spine. So, to compensate, she cooed sweetly,

'As a wedding gift from Daddy, I'd say not,' and saw stark, killing anger look out from amber eyes before he shuttered them with a veil of indifference, adding blandly, as if totally unaware of her barbed remark,

'And it does have a huge plus sign in its favour.'

'Only one?' Tolly grinned, obviously gratified because his choice had found favour, beginning to walk towards the parked limo, the chauffeur already folding away the paper he'd been reading.

'The outbuildings. With a little modification they would make an ideal set-up for the agency.' A small sideways glance in Imogen's direction was the first indication since their earlier confrontation that he was aware of her presence. 'But we can talk that through at some later date.'

But Tolly was having none of that. 'Spit it out now. We can look them over more closely while we're here and be done with it. No sense in making a special journey out again.'

Not even Alex could deny the sense in that, but the look he gave Imogen as she blithely tacked along would have withered a less hardy spirit.

'Perhaps Miss Paige would prefer to sit this out, wait in the car?' he suggested, stony-faced.

But Tolly put in immediately, smiling into her eyes because, so far, no one but himself and Imogen knew she had a legitimate interest in where the new agency would be situated, 'Certainly not. I want

Imogen right along with us on this.' And she found herself on the receiving end of a look of contemptuous hostility that she should have found intolerable but which made her gulp hurriedly, swallowing laughter.

She was beginning to enjoy herself thoroughly. Getting under his skin was a wicked pleasure and something she had never experienced before. And she listened to all that was said, inserting a few comments of her own. With a few structural alterations the premises would be ideal.

'Save a bomb on the type of rent being asked for office premises in the City.' Alex was well in his stride, both men exhibiting a direct and cutting quality when it came down to the nitty-gritty of business, and she might have said he'd forgotten her presence except for the almost visible charge of awareness in the air.

'There's a good main-line service to and from the City, and I dare say we could recruit all the secretarial help we need from Windsor itself.' Alex was looking out of one of the huge windows that made the rooms so ideally light and airy, and he added, 'I've spoken to Pierre Vinet and he's enthusiastic about coming over to us.'

'He's one of the best visuals men in the business, and is employed by the agency we've used for Devenko's Paris up until now,' Tolly explained for Imogen's benefit, and Alex went right on, as if the little exchange hadn't happened.

'I don't know how you feel about it, but I think he's the right guy to head the agency. His English is fluent and he knows the ins and outs of admin pretty well considering the magnitude of his talents on the creative side.'

'I'd like him on the team; his was one of the names we mentioned in our earlier discussions,' Tolly said, and Imogen held her breath. She knew what was coming and was waiting to see Alex Devenko explode.

'But I've offered Imogen the job. If she'll accept, I want her to head the new promotion team.'

He didn't explode. He seemed to freeze, his golden eyes narrowed as they bored into her soul. But there was anger there, silent and intense, all the more deadly for being contained. And she knew exactly how to get her revenge for all those disgusting insults. And she took it.

'Tolly, I accept. I'd love to take the job.' And was rewarded by his beaming smile, his enthusiastic hand-clasp.

She was on a high, the impulsiveness of her decision, the reason for it, not hitting her then. The silence coming from Alex Devenko was almost deafening and she was listening to it, revelling in the heady sensation of triumph, taken off balance when he said quietly, darkly,

'I see. My congratulations, Miss Paige.' And his narrowed eyes told her he'd like to kill her on the spot and she could have laughed in his face until he turned to the older man, his tone easy and languid now as he said, 'I suggest I run Miss Paige back to the City. If she's about to join Devenko's I'd like to get to know her better. I'm sure you can manage without her company just this once, and I know we have a lot to discuss.'

Only she could detect the hidden nuances in his words and as Tolly said, smiling broadly, 'Sure, go ahead. But don't break any speed records in that bullet of yours; I like my staff to stay in one piece,' she felt a ripple of something remarkably akin to terror run over her skin.

Apart from protesting, making a scene, making herself look an utter fool in front of the new boss she had suddenly and impulsively acquired, there was nothing she could do about the altered travelling arrangements.

It was one thing deliberately to needle the man when his father was around to offer some protection from his verbal assaults, his open threats. To be alone with him, locked in the confines of his car, would be quite a different scene!

CHAPTER THREE

AND it was. Leaving Tolly to return to London at a more sedate pace in the chauffeur-driven limo, the Jaguar snarled its way through the busy Windsor streets like a leashed but dangerous animal.

Alex didn't speak and when Imogen glanced at him his profile was grim, his mouth pulled into a tight line. She couldn't think of a thing to say. In the face of his icy hostility, the brooding power that surrounded him like an aura, filling the confines of the racy car, anything she could say would come out sounding inadequate, she knew it would.

She was edgy, her fingers curled into the palms of her hands, and she knew she should try to put the record straight—to tell him that Tolly had offered her the job on merit alone, that their friendship had developed because they had found they had a lot in common, could talk easily to each other on any subject under the sun, that she wished her own father could have been more like him.

She had enjoyed playing up to his conception of her, sending his blood-pressure rocketing, but she had had the protection of Tolly's presence then, and now, alone with the grim-faced devil, she didn't really think it wise to carry on with the charade.

Besides, she excused her sudden cowardice, it would be gratifying to wrest an apology from the brute. And they were going to have to work with each other, perhaps not closely, but, even so, closely enough to make a continuation of this type of hostility unwise.

Common sense was winning the day and she was all set to begin her explanation when, hitting the motorway, Alex put his foot on the accelerator and drawled, 'Where's it to be? Your place or mine?' He subjected her to a brief, brooding stare. 'Things are even worse than I thought. I didn't know you'd added a high-profile job to your shopping-list. Does the thought of having power turn you on?' His sensual mouth curled with distaste. 'We have a lot of talking to do, and I think you'll find I can be very persuasive.'

Common sense, all thoughts of trying to make him see things as they were and not as his twisted mind imagined them to be, fled out of Imogen's head like a snowflake in a heat wave, and she dragged in an angry breath and clipped right back, 'You might think you're God Almighty, but nothing you could do or say would persuade me to give up a plum of a job offer, or end my friendship with your father!'

How dared he sit in judgement, treat her like the piece of dirt he had obviously decided her to be? She'd see him in hell before she put his mind at rest and told him the truth of the situation!

Staring straight ahead, she braced herself for his anger, telling herself she could handle anything he cared to throw at her. He made her furious enough to cope with the worst he could come up with!

But the expected insults and tongue-lashing didn't come. If anything, he sounded almost indifferent as he stated,

'We'll see. The handful of people who have underestimated me in the past have lived to regret it. You're not going to be any different.'

The powerful car was eating the miles. They had left the motorway at Chiswick and as they approached Hammersmith he asked again, 'Your place or mine?'

She snapped, 'Get lost! Drop me anywhere here; I can find my own way home.'

She'd rather walk a hundred miles than stay in his insulting presence a moment longer, but he said equably,

'If you won't give me your address it will have to be my hotel,' and that had her blurting out the name of her street in Shepherd's Bush, the apartment building. If he insisted on 'persuading' her to leave his father alone she would rather be on her own home ground.

As she slotted her door-key into the lock she had to will herself to stay calm. His dark presence, right behind her, threatened to overwhelm her. She didn't doubt his statement that people who underestimated him lived to regret it. But she wasn't going to grovel, to beg him to believe her innocent of the charge of gold-digging. He could be the one to beg—and begging her forgiveness would do for starters!

As a place to live her apartment was modest. With rents as high as they were in London she couldn't afford anything grander. And, as if picking up her thought waves, he looked around the small, uncluttered living-room and, thrusting his hands into his trouser pockets, rocked back on his heels and drawled,

'I'd have thought you could have taken him for something more suitable to your expensive image. Or are you still working on it?'

As she tossed her small leather handbag on to a chair, Imogen's face went white. She was tired of the insults, of the entire farce. The mischievous enjoyment she'd gained from allowing him to believe his own black fantasy had suddenly turned sour and she said wearily, 'Do you always believe everything you read in the papers?' and turned to face him, her eyes dark and enormous against the pallor of her skin.

'In this particular instance, yes.' The look he gave her was insultingly sexual, taking her breath away, and she folded her arms tightly in front of her because any minute now she might just hit him and he would hit her back. He was that kind of brute.

He gave her a grim stare, a frown-line appearing between his brooding golden eyes as he admitted curtly, 'You worry me. I'd have staked my life on Tolly's business sense. He's too wily to allow a beautiful face and body to come between him and his judgement where Devenko's is concerned—or so I would have believed. But you've only to ask for a prestigious and important job to get it. He must be losing his marbles.'

'And you wouldn't believe me if I told you he'd offered me the job on merit?' she accused quietly, sinking down on a squashy sofa, the dark navy up-holstery making her hair look like silver spun silk.

And he bit out, 'No, I would not,' as she had known he would, and she lifted her shoulders in a slight shrug, no longer prepared to waste her breath in her own defence. He would only believe the truth when it came from Tolly.

As Tolly himself had told her, the idea for a single agency, promoting Devenko's worldwide, had been his brainchild. He'd been keeping his eyes wide open, looking for the ideal team to use when the time came to put the project in motion. And he'd been impressed by the 'Jewels' promotion, by the flair and quality of the campaigns, had made it his business to find out who had been primarily re-sponsible, had offered her the job...

'So how much would it take?' He was standing over her, his face set, the line of his wide shoulders very rigid, and Imogen stared at him, not understanding.

His mouth then curled as he said derisively, 'The look of wide-eyed innocence won't wash. Don't pretend you don't know what I'm talking about.' He came to sit beside her, taking her chin in one steel-hard hand, forcing her to meet his dep-recating eyes. 'Walk away from the job, and from Tolly, and you can name your price.'

She shuddered beneath his insolent gaze, her breath catching in her lungs as his fingers began stroking the long, pure line of her throat.

Sensations that had nothing to do with his latest appalling insult shivered through her and her soft lips parted as she tried to understand what in the world was happening to her. It was like nothing she had ever experienced before, a sensation that was as mindless as it was debilitating. Apart from being the most arrogant, the plain nastiest male she had ever encountered, he was also the sexiest, and the implications of that revelation were terrifying . . .

'Speechless with cupidity? Or are you still trying to work out how much you can take me for?'

That rich, dark voice had been one of the first things she had noticed about him; it was mesmeric, fascinating, and it was that, the effect of it, Imogen fought against as she suddenly twisted her head away.

But his hands grasped her shoulders, his fingers biting through the soft fabric of her jacket, and there was no escape, no escape at all as he got to his feet, pulling her with him, her body brushing against his in slight, erotic contact. And his eyes burned into hers, and the colour was hot and alive, and she knew what he was thinking before he recognised it himself.

She watched the perception come in the utter stillness of mental recoil, the flicker of distaste that darkened his eyes, the hardening of his mouth that came just an infinitesimal moment before he abruptly released her, turning, asking tersely, 'Do your housekeeping skills run to anything as exotic as coffee?'

She knew he was ruffled. Knew why. He, too, had felt the strange and unstoppable effect of sexual chemistry and it appalled him. Just as it had appalled her. Hadn't it?

They were even again, the score level. In that, at least, he was floundering as much as she.

And that was responsible for the sudden high she was on, she informed herself as she went through to the kitchen to make coffee. The hard man, too, had moments when his control slipped. It was good to know.

But he was in complete control again when she carried the tray through, putting it down on the oblong table at the side of the easy-chair he had taken. And he took the cup she offered him with nothing more than a brief dip of his handsome head and his voice was remote as he told her,

'Name your price and make yourself scarce, or suffer the consequences. And don't make the mistake of thinking I'm not serious.' He stirred his coffee absently, his intent eyes never leaving her face, and she couldn't believe that any man in his right mind could, on the strength of one trashy snippet in a trashy gossip column, have her condemned without a hearing.

Not that she had exactly pressed for a hearing, she reminded herself honestly; she'd been too busy stringing him along, letting him stew because of the insults he'd handed out.

Sighing, she took her coffee over to the window and stared out. It was already beginning to grow dusk and the view of the street wasn't inspiring, but she couldn't bear to witness the way he was watching her, as if he could see right through her and didn't like what he found.

She would have to make him understand that she had no designs on his father. Never had, never would have. And, her back still to him, she began, 'I don't know why you're so uptight over the idea of Tolly becoming involved with a younger woman,' and knew she'd said exactly the wrong thing, reinforced his unsavoury opinion of her, when she heard his sudden, muttered oath. He hadn't given her the opportunity to finish what she'd intended to say, which was, 'It's fine if he becomes romantically involved—he's not exactly over the hill yet—only it won't be with me.'

She heard the crash as he replaced his cup on the saucer, and opened her mouth to finish what she'd been saying, but the phone rang out, filling the thick silence, and she went to it quickly, her heart hammering because she could feel his hatred of her clear across the room.

And she listened while Tolly said, 'I can't trace Alex, so you'll be the first to know. The deal's gone through. Devenko's London is all systems go! Have dinner with me tonight and we'll celebrate. And I'll want your ideas on the feasibility of using those buildings as a studio. OK? After all, you'll be the one who's running the show and, if you'd prefer something more central, it's yours. I'll send the car to pick you up in an hour.'

She replaced the receiver slowly, carefully. She would have dinner with Tolly if only to get him to straighten things out. Alex would listen to him. There was no way he would listen to her.

And when she turned she found his narrowed eyes on her and her wretched heart picked up speed again, knocking against her ribs, and he must have listened to her end of the conversation, arriving at the right conclusion, because he said with quiet menace, 'You're seeing Tolly tonight,' and got smoothly to his feet, his amber eyes on her face. 'So be it.'

And it was like a declaration of war and she knew intuitively that what had gone before would be as nothing when compared to what was to come. He walked to the door and let himself out, and there'd been no expression on his unforgettable features, nothing to tell her what was going on in his clever, devious mind.

Suddenly, Imogen felt icy cold.

'Another beautiful evening, miss.' The chauffeur handed her into the back of the limo and Imogen smiled and said yes, it was, although she hadn't really thought about it, her mind too full of her increasingly awful confrontations with the overbearing Alex Devenko to take in anything else.

It was a clear evening, not even a breath of wind, the still air chilly. There would probably be a slight frost later, the first of the season, and she snuggled gratefully into the warmth of the lightweight white cashmere jacket she wore over a black wool-knit tapered sheath.

She hadn't had time to do much about her hair and had opted to leave it loose, caught back with a wide tortoiseshell clip at the nape of her neck and, as the car purred through the streets towards Kensington and Tolly's small but very exclusive hotel, she told herself to calm down.

It had been a rush to get ready in time, and her mind had been too occupied with the bitter antagonism between herself and Alex to think ahead to this evening. She was going to have to let Tolly know what was going on inside his son's head. Tactfully. She didn't want to cause bad feeling between father and son. And she was going to have to ask the older man to convince the younger that their relationship was above board. Otherwise, working for Devenko's would become not only the greatest challenge she had ever faced but damn nigh impossible!

Pausing outside Tolly's suite, she took a deep breath, pinned a smile on her face and put her finger on the bell. The door opened immediately and Tolly was there, looking reassuringly ordinary, normal, his still-handsome face wreathed in a smile of welcome. And her own smile widened as he caught her to him in a friendly bear-hug. She was used to his expansive gestures by now, the openly expressed warmth of his fiery Ukrainian ancestry.

And a voice, cool and deadly, slid between them, 'Let me take your coat, Miss Paige,' and Imogen groaned inwardly, her stomach doing a nose-dive, lurching upwards again to lodge somewhere behind her breastbone.

What the hell was he doing here? If he planned on hanging around, then her chances of having a quiet word with Tolly were nil.

But he was wearing a dinner-jacket, black tie, looking spectacularly devastating, so maybe he was going on somewhere. She most sincerely hoped so . . .

'What's with this formality, my boy?' Tolly chided as Imogen slipped her arms out of her jacket

and handed it to Alex before he could come to help
her. She didn't want him near her, let alone touching
her, and Tolly was saying, 'As of this afternoon,
Imogen's one of the team.'

Alex said drily, 'Almost one of the family.'

'Absolutely!' Tolly had a blind spot where
undercurrents were concerned but, as he didn't
know of his son's disgusting suspicions, she couldn't
really blame him.

And Alex countered, his rich voice dark and soft,
'Then I must welcome her appropriately,' and
reached out his arms to pull her supple body against
his impeccable length, his dark head bent until his
sensual mouth was a mere breath away from hers.
And he paused, just a moment, intense amber eyes
glittering into startled violet, before his mouth
covered hers, the gentle, inescapable contact un-
believably erotic, sending convulsions of sensation
to cavort wildly through her bloodstream.

And then he released her, leaving her shattered,
her lips still parted as though begging for more,
and her face crawled with colour as she realised
how she must look. Then Tolly said 'Bravo', his
voice cracking with laughter, and everything was
back to normal again. Or almost so.

The devil had taken her by surprise, that was all.
Throughout the day she had grown used to his insults and had recognised that, until Tolly could put
him straight, she would simply have to put up with
them.

That sensual embrace had been entirely unexpected, knocking her off balance, that was all, she
consoled herself as Tolly handed her a flute of

sparkling Dom Perignon and she lifted the glass to his toast of 'Devenko's London, and the new agency', and found herself looking into Alexsander's glinting eyes. She felt the smile leave her lips, leave them trembling.

'Then to business, but gently!' Tolly smiled as he joined her on the Regency-style sofa. The living area of the suite was decorated and furnished in mock-Regency and baroque, elegant to look at but not top of the league in the comfort stakes, she thought, as Alex swivelled round a spindly, gilded chair and straddled it. She wished he would stop looking at her with those cold golden eyes, the smile that came so softly, so readily now, never quite reaching them.

After the earlier open hostilities this new approach unnerved her. His being here at all unnerved her. She couldn't understand him. She didn't want to understand him because, if she did, she might find herself, against all logic, actually beginning to like him!

'Now,' Tolly began, crossing his legs at the ankles and leaning back, turning his paternal smile on Imogen. 'I would like to see the agency off and running by the new year, which would mean your giving in your notice to Martin and Sandown straight away. And, in the interim, you won't be idle.' He grinned mischievously, tipping his iron-grey head on one side. 'You'll have a team to get together, you'll need to visit all the other stores— which, incidentally, you'll have to do in any case, on a fairly regular basis. There will be secretaries to be hired, hardware to be installed—which brings me to the question of premises.' He lifted an eyebrow in the direction of his watchful son. 'I know Alex favours Windsor, but do you?'

Imogen would have given a great deal to disagree, to put her foot down and show the high and mighty one that even though he was head of Devenko's in all but name he couldn't have things all his own way. But common sense prevailed. The Windsor premises were ideal and would cut down overheads. The exclusive chain of stores wasn't exactly out with the begging-bowl but to throw money away needlessly was senseless.

She gave a tiny sigh, which she hoped no one heard, and said, 'Yes,' then voiced a question which had been hovering in the back of her mind ever since she'd impulsively accepted the job. 'Will the London agency be responsible for advertising in the States? I don't think it was made clear during our previous discussions.'

There were six stores, all occupying prestigious sites in six major North American cities, quite apart from those in Europe, and Tolly glanced across at Alex before telling her, 'In principle, yes. At the moment Alex oversees the US campaigns. There was, shall we say——' he spread his hands '—a difference of opinion between our advertising director and the rest of the board. He is no longer with us, so Alex, along with his other duties, supervises the various promotions, Stateside. However——' again the slightly defiant look in the direction of his son '—once you have found your feet—as I am confident you will quickly do—you will be entirely responsible for all Devenko advertising, world-wide—and have a place on the board.'

Imogen gulped involuntarily. This was more, far more, than she had bargained for. And, grasping at her poise, she lifted her eyes to gauge Alex's reaction. He would be furious to think his father's mistress was being handed a directorship, a place on the board of the exclusive family business. His teeth would be curling with rage!

But he was still smiling, and the smile was pleasant, and that shook her because, believing what he believed, he had to be furious at what he'd just heard. And Tolly went on, his puzzled eyes resting on his son, as if he, too, had expected some objections at this juncture.

'In fact, Alex will have definite ideas of his own and express them ferociously—he always does. So you might find yourself with a fight on your hands from time to time, and you will, of course, to begin with at least, be working closely together.'

'I think we can handle that,' Alex put in, his smile widening, his eyes making a lazy visual exploration of her body beneath the soft, clinging fabric of her dress. 'In fact, I think I shall rather enjoy it. How about you, Imogen?'

Was he referring to possible clashes over the US advertising, or to the fact that they would appear to need to work closely together for a time? Who could tell? So she just smiled, her face feeling tight, her mind racing as she tried to work out what he was up to.

But the arrival of a waiter with their meal and a fresh bottle of champagne stopped that particular and unwelcome train of conversation and the three of them talked of neutral topics while the gilded table in the window alcove was deftly laid, the candles lit.

And Tolly led her to the table, seated her, but after that Alex took over, and if she hadn't known better she would have said he was flirting with her over the black Russian caviare and buckwheat blinis, the spicy chicken Bangkok.

As far as Alex appeared to be concerned Tolly scarcely existed. He spoke to her alone, his eyes were for her alone, and, by the time a delicious confection of vanilla ice-cream smothered with hot butterscotch sauce was put in front of her, her head was reeling.

Alexsander Devenko, at his most charming, was potent indeed and she hadn't missed the way Tolly watched them, his dark eyes puzzled, the faintest of frown-lines pulling his brows together. She gave him a wry smile across the table. He couldn't possibly be as puzzled as she!

And Alex said softly, 'About your flat in Shepherd's Bush—the new job will involve you in a lot of travelling, initially, a lot of hard graft. Won't you find commuting out to Windsor a grind?'

Imogen shook her head. She'd been thinking about that. One way or another, her acceptance of the post with Devenko's had provided her with more than a little food for thought.

'I'm not particularly fond of where I live, but it was the best I could run to when I moved from Lincoln to take up my job with Martin and

Sandown. I might look for somewhere in Windsor.' Although Alex had asked the question she looked at Tolly as she answered. Alex had effectively excluded him from the conversation for the past hour, and she was beginning to feel sorry for him.

And he beamed, 'That's a great idea!' and Alex countered smoothly,

'I've got a better one. Use the flat above the stable-block; you'd be right on hand.' He leaned back in his chair, idly refilling Imogen's glass with the crisp champagne, his smile courteous, urbane. 'You've no objections, Father?'

There was a tiny silence. Tiny but very intense. Imogen could actually hear the champagne bubbles fizzing in her glass. Then Tolly said, 'No, none at all,' very quickly, and she knew he was feeling out of his depth. So was she. And because she knew his rosy plans for that particular part of the property he fully intended to buy—to install a housekeeper-gardener couple because Catrina wasn't all that domesticated—she objected mildly,

'Thanks for the offer, but I'll have to think about it. And in the meantime I'll see what's going in Windsor itself.'

She took a sip of the cold champagne then put the glass down quickly. She was already feeling completely disorientated without taking in any more alcohol. Everything had happened so quickly. Alex's foul accusations, his insults, her impulsive acceptance of a job she'd promised to give herself more time to think over—a direct response to his clearly voiced scathing opinion of her, and her own need to score points off him. And on top of all that there was his sudden and inexplicable change of attitude. Everything, quite suddenly, began to seem too much, and when Tolly said, 'It's been quite a day, Imogen. Would you like me to ring down for the car?' she could only smile in weary gratitude, longing for the privacy of her own little patch, the opportunity to unwind and view the events of the day with her customary cool detachment.

'No need. I'll drive Imogen home.' Alex was on his feet, a proprietorial hand beneath her elbow as he helped her from the table. 'After all, her acceptance of the position you offered her means we're going to be very close colleagues indeed.' The grin he showed his father was tigerish. 'And, if the partnership's going to work—and I intend that it will— I'm going to have to get to know her a great deal better.'

His hand had slid up across her back, very slowly, very deliberately, and it rested against her shoulder now, his long fingers circling, moulding her flesh with an almost shocking intimacy, and her blood ran with fire, throbbing through her veins, the unwanted contact doing strange things to her equilibrium. And her eyes were wide with shock as she glanced at the older man, noticed his sudden frown, and she opened her mouth to protest, to say she would rather the chauffeur drove her home, but Alex was in there first, his voice slightly mocking as he asked, 'Any objections, Tolly?' his confident smile, the arrogant way he held his head proclaiming that it wouldn't matter a damn if he had.

And Tolly answered gruffly, his shrewd brown eyes startled, 'No. Go ahead. I'll see you in the morning. There are a few things we need to discuss.'

And Imogen felt her face burn. The older man was no fool; he must have seen how Alex had treated her for the major part of the evening—as if she were the only woman in the world. And he couldn't have avoided seeing how Alex's touch had affected her.

Alex had been flirting with her practically all evening, eating her with his eyes, and Alex was engaged to Catrina, the girl Tolly had hand-picked. Tolly had no way of knowing that Alex loathed and despised her, believed she was out for all she could get—and that included a seat on the board!

Suddenly, she felt icy cold, as if she had been plunged into a deep, dark sea and couldn't swim. She was a pawn in some devious game Alexsander Devenko was playing, and, if she weren't very careful, or very clever, he would annihilate her completely!

CHAPTER FOUR

THE drive to Imogen's flat didn't take long and the events of the evening had drained her of energy. Crossing swords with Alexsander Devenko demanded an energy she just didn't have at the moment, while he, damn him, seemed to have an inexhaustible supply.

So she kept quiet, kept her fingers crossed, hoping he would simply drop her off outside the building and allow her to crawl away into her flat and try to get the day's events into some kind of perspective. Right at this moment she needed her own space, needed it with weary desperation.

'I'll see you in,' he stated as he pulled the Jaguar up in front of her apartment building, and she said, trying to sound relaxed about it,

'There's really no need,' and unbuckled her seatbelt with shaky fingers, hoping against hope that he would let the matter rest.

But he didn't, of course, and she ground her teeth with frustration as he exited the car, locked it and was round at her side with a smooth speed that boded ill for any further objections she might make.

And why object? she thought logically. His presence this evening had meant that she hadn't had the opportunity to tell Tolly how that newspaper article had sparked off a violent reaction in his son, made him believe that she was nothing but a cheap little gold-digger, intent on milking the older man of all she could get. A few words from Tolly would have put the record straight, convinced Alex of the truth.

'I'll make coffee,' she told him as he followed her into her tiny sitting-room, and make you listen to the truth, she added in her head as he smiled into her eyes, his own eyes a warm caress that sent a wayward shudder rippling through her.

Stiffening her spine, she walked quickly away. He knew how to make a girl go weak at the knees and, the worst thing was, the devil knew it!

Perhaps his ability to turn on the charm whenever it suited him was the real reason behind Catrina's objections to naming the day. No wife would want to stand by and see other women flocking around her husband whenever he crooked a finger in their direction, she thought acidly as she closed the door of her cramped kitchen behind her and began to put grounds into the filter machine.

But his forthcoming marriage was no business of hers, she informed herself tartly. Her only concern was to make him believe the truth regarding herself and Tolly. And that only because the truth, and a proper understanding, would open the way for a smoother working relationship.

When she carried the tray through he was investigating the books on the shelves she'd had built and he'd discarded his jacket, as if he found even the low level of central heating too much. She could see the breadth of his rangy shoulders beneath the crisp white lawn, the powerful musculature clearly delineated, his back tapering down to a taut waist-line, narrow hips...

She looked away quickly, putting the tray down on the table with a clatter, schooling her features to impassivity, willing her racing pulses to settle down to normal because the chemistry between them, compounded of suspicion and distrust, un-willing sexual attraction, made a potentially explosive equation.

He turned, a slow smile lapped his cruelly sensual mouth and he said, 'How very nice,' and she didn't know whether he was referring to the coffee or to her; but he made himself clear, very clear, when he added softly, his rich dark voice, as ever, making her come out in goose-bumps,

'I'm always delighted when a beautiful woman invites me to her rooms late at night on the pretext of coffee.'

Fighting off the mesmeric spell of that beautiful voice, the intimate caress of those golden eyes, Imogen tried to get her head together enough to explain that he'd got it all wrong, as usual, that her reason for asking him in for coffee was very dif-ferent from the one he obviously had in mind! But he paced towards her, his very movements seductive.

'Take off that coat. It's stifling in here.'

Her wide eyes flew to his and her fingers clutched the edges of her jacket together defensively. The room was airless, but she was suddenly and pain-fully aware of how the black, fine-knit sheath she was wearing clung so lovingly to her slender curves.

'Let me,' he said, his voice taunting, and the shiver she gave as he gently began to unfurl her fingers brought a knowing smile to his lips, and he was close now, their bodies almost touching as he slid the white jacket off her shoulders and dropped it unceremoniously on to a chair.

And then his hands went to unfasten the tortoiseshell clip that held her hair neatly in place, his fingers drifting through the long, silver-blonde tresses, and she muttered, 'Don't,' her voice low and husky, and he looked deep into her wide, bewildered eyes, and she knew that something was beginning, was growing, and had to be stopped.

Things were getting out of hand, but she had precious little experience to draw on to help her. The idea of casual sex left a nasty taste in her mouth and the idea of something more permanent, a long-term relationship or marriage, had never found a place in her head. Her childhood had been spent on the battleground of her parents' marriage. It had been enough to put her off that state for life.

Pulling herself together, trying to shut out the sight of that curving, sensual mouth so close to her own, she pulled away a little and tried to achieve a brisk tone.

'About that article—Tolly and me——' and he placed a finger against her lips, pushing her breath back into her throat.

'I don't want to hear about it.'

And then his mouth covered hers, softly at first, caressing the curve of her lips, parting them with a gentle expertise that undermined her defences, leaving her prey to the insidious pressure of a sensual need she had never experienced before. And, as his kiss deepened, his arms pulling her pliant body close into his, her heart began to beat so rapidly that she thought it would burst out of her body.

Awareness of the heat of his thighs tight against hers made her bones turn to water and she knew this was wrong, so very wrong, but could do nothing to stem the inexorable flow of blind physical need. Easier to stop the flow of an ocean's tide.

Mindlessly, her arms twined around his neck and she felt her breasts crushed against the hard wall of his chest as his arms tightened around her; and she felt his tongue brush hers in an intimate caress and knew that, for her, nothing would ever be the same again. And she said his name, softly, on a dying sigh, their breath mingling, and she heard him groan, deep in his throat, before lifting his head, his hands moving to gently cup her face.

His golden eyes were glazed with desire, the skin across his taut cheekbones flushed dull red. And he said thickly, 'I've been wanting to do that since I first saw you. You looked cool and perfect, and I wanted you.'

And her languorous violet 'yes' told him that she, too, had wants and needs, emotions that he, with his velvet voice and amber eyes, had called into being, and, still cradling her head, his hard male hands on either side of her face, he brushed his lips lightly over hers, just once, and told her wryly,

'Yes, I know. I know, pet.' And put her gently away from him. 'And now, I think, I should be wise and go.' He hooked his discarded jacket over his shoulder by his thumb and his smile was mocking. And whether the mockery was for himself, or for her, she didn't know. All she knew, as he walked out of the door, was that her life would never seem quite the same again.

Morning brought sense. Well, almost sense. She still felt shaky as she got up, showered, and made coffee.

But a certain amount of shakiness, a feeling of wateriness in her bones, was only to be expected after an initiation into the world of passion, she informed herself staunchly.

Her feelings about emotional relationships had meant that she had put her career before her personal life, wanting to carve a secure niche for herself in her chosen profession because she had known very little security in childhood.

One of her parents had always been on the point of leaving the other, only staying together—or so they told other people—because of the child. And that had made Imogen feel like a heavy, unwanted burden.

When they had finally divorced, during her first year in college, she had felt nothing but relief. Since she had been put off the relationship between the sexes, the men she had dated had never been permitted to advance beyond a chaste kiss. So she had never before experienced the havoc of sexual need.

Her initiation, coming, probably, ten years later than normal, had been more shattering because of it, as a childhood illness was more devastating if contracted in later life.

She finished her coffee and went back to her bedroom to dress, choosing a charcoal suit with a faint pin-stripe over a cherry-red blouse. Sheer black silk stockings and red high heels completed her outfit and she pulled her hair back into a French pleat and felt almost herself again.

Today she would go into her office at Martin and Sandown and type out her notice. She was looking forward to starting with Devenko's. It would be an enormous challenge and she would enjoy rising to it. And if Alexsander Devenko ever laid another finger on her she would slap his head off.

Sometimes, if she couldn't see her way clearly, perhaps over a decision to be made, she would make lists. Pros and cons, and it always worked. But she didn't need to make a list to tell her that all she felt for Alex was plain, old-fashioned lust, a stirring of the senses that had lain dormant for so long that they had almost become atrophied.

And she didn't even like the man. Or did she? Anyway, like him or not, nothing altered the fact that he saw her as a mercenary little gold-digger, out to get her hands on his father's money and a seat on the board of Devenko's.

Besides, he was heavily engaged to another woman and... She sat down abruptly on the stool in front of her dressing-table and watched her violet eyes narrow, her full lips tighten into a straight line.

So that was it. And why hadn't she thought of it before? His whole attitude had changed as soon as he'd realised his father intended to give her a seat on the board, eventually. He had started to flirt with her, had insisted on taking her home—

and all for his father's benefit. Threats and offers of a pay-off hadn't worked and so, he would have reasoned, he would try an assault on her senses, take her away from the older man by the sheer force of his fantastically potent male sexuality. And that, if nothing else, would demonstrate to Tolly precisely what a little tramp she was!

Clever, she thought, a reluctantly admiring glint showing deep in her eyes. But not clever enough. If she had been the tramp of his warped imaginings, then she might well have ditched the older man in favour of whatever the younger might offer.

But she wasn't a tramp, and he'd get to know that in time. Meanwhile, she had an old job to dispose of and a new one to begin. She stood up, her shoulders straight, hooked her bag over her shoulder by its long, slender strap, and marched out.

It was early afternoon when she returned and the phone was ringing, and Tolly said, 'So I've caught you at last! Where've you been?'

'Handing in my notice and clearing my desk,' and phoning round estate agents after suitable pads in Windsor, she tacked on in her head.

And Tolly said warmly, 'Good girl. There'll be a contract in the post to you in a few days' time. If there's anything you don't agree with, have a word with Alex; he'll get it sorted out.'

'And when do I start work for you?' Imogen hooked a chair towards her with her foot and sat down, easing her shoes off.

And Tolly told her expansively, 'As far as I'm concerned, you're on the payroll as of now. But

take things easy for the next few weeks. We employ
people to do the donkey work, such as physically
setting up the Windsor premises. We'll need to get
planning permission, of course, but our legal boys
will push that through as soon as the property
changes hands. So all you need to do for the next
few weeks is relax a little, build up your strength!
Oh, and take a trip to Paris with Alex. He's setting
up a meeting with the guys who will make up your
team.'

Imogen's heart performed a peculiar, sinking
somersault at that, but she was too professional to
voice any objections. Meeting the other team
members, drawn, apparently, from various parts
of the Continent as well as the UK, would be
invaluable when it came to actually working together in Windsor. Much better than a completely
cold start.

'Oh, and before I forget, I've talked it over with
Alex and we both agree that you should use the flat
above the stables. At least to begin with, while
you're getting the agency into full swing.'

It did make sense. Her exploratory calls to
various estate agents had established that suitable
properties, for lease or rent in and around Windsor,
were as rare as rainfall in the desert. And she didn't
relish the thought of travelling from Shepherd's
Bush each day. But she did remind him, 'What
about the live-over-the-stables-housekeeper idea,
when your son marries?'

And, after a short but very intense silence, Tolly
said quickly, 'I shouldn't worry your head about
that, if I were you. And, talking about that son of

mine, he's been trying to contact you all morning, too—seems he's got something planned for the two of you this evening.'

Oh, has he? Imogen thought, gritting her teeth. They'd see about that! Then she frowned as Tolly told her,

'I'll be in the States for the next couple of weeks, while the sale of the Windsor house goes through. Just phoned to let you know I won't be around for a while, but I'll expect you at the house-warming!'

'I'll miss you,' she said, meaning it. Her friendship with Tolly had begun to mean a lot to her, and he chuckled.

'Good. It's been a long time since a pretty girl missed me! But something cropped up, which, so Alex insists, only I can handle. Don't believe a word of it myself. But when Alex insists, he insists!'

Neither did she, Imogen thought as she put down the receiver. Alex had been busy. Very busy. Manoeuvring Tolly out of harm's way, out of the clutches of a predatory gold-digger!

She sighed, wondering what his devious mind would come up with next. He'd obviously decided that the strategy of the night before, using his charm and his obvious sexuality to take her away from a much older man, wouldn't work.

Wrinkling her brow, she picked up her discarded shoes and went to her bedroom to change into something more casual. Come to think of it, it had been Alex who had called a halt last night. She'd been lost in the sensual world he'd created and couldn't have stopped a single damn thing.

The knowledge, besides giving her a *frisson* of deep shame, gave her food for thought. And it wasn't very palatable food, either.

He'd probably found making love to her hard work. When push had come to shove he'd found he didn't fancy her. Maybe he'd had Catrina on his mind, decided that she, Imogen, came a very poor second best. For some reason, as she stripped off her clothes and rummaged in a drawer for fresh underwear, a light sweater and a pair of well-washed jeans, she felt extraordinarily desolate.

CHAPTER FIVE

'I THINK that just about wraps it up,' Alex said, gathering his papers together and stacking them tidily on the polished table-top in front of him. 'Unless anyone has any more questions?'

Imogen glanced around, a small, satisfied smile on her full lips. Apart from herself and Alex, there were three other people around the table—the team Alex and Tolly had hand-picked to run the Devenko agency.

This was their second day in Paris, and what Imogen had fully expected to be an ordeal had turned out to be an exciting experience. The enthusiasm and willingness to co-operate on the part of the others had impressed her. And there was, she recognised, a great deal of collective talent gathered in the superb hotel suite. They were young and hungry for success, and working with them was going to be a joy.

But the deep enjoyment of these past two days had to be down, in part, to Alex, she admitted honestly. After Tolly's unexpected departure to the States, four weeks ago, she had quite deliberately avoided him, because, without Tolly to act as a buffer, she knew she would find Alex difficult to handle.

So she had made herself scarce, her daytimes spent working out her notice, her evenings holed away with her girlfriends, dreading the day when she and Alex would depart from Gatwick for the conference he had set up in Paris.

And the day had come and she was free of Martin and Sandown, but full of apprehension, and on her way to Paris to meet her future colleagues. Would Alex treat her with the insulting contempt she'd had to endure when she'd first met him? Or would he continue with that puzzling and dangerous flirtation?

Both prospects alarmed her.

She had to endure neither. From the outset he had treated her with warmth and friendliness, and, what was more, as a respected colleague. And after a few hours she had given up trying to figure him out. The man, and his moods, was an enigma. Better to simply enjoy the mood of the moment and be thankful.

'I think we've discussed every possible angle.' Pierre Vinet, a highly gifted visuals man poached from one of the top Paris agencies, lobbed a smile around the table. He was dark and wiry with intense black eyes and hair, but when he smiled his thin features lit up with Gallic charm.

Imogen had been afraid that he might resent her for taking the top position when he must have known that he had been Alex's first choice for the job. But so far no such chauvinistic vibes had trickled through. He had even complimented her on the 'Jewels' campaign with so much sincerity that she had actually blushed. So she smiled right back at him and said,

'Sorry to sound a prosaic note, but there is the question of accommodation to be gone into.'

Cathy Ames, the young and promising copy-writer from a Manchester agency, who would work directly with Imogen, said pertly, 'I'm fixed up. Luckily, I've got an aunt living in Ascot; she's offered to put me up. And I've just bought a second-hand Metro, so getting to work won't be any problem.'

Which left Pierre and Stefan Stein. Stefan was a brilliant all-rounder, spoke fluent Italian and Spanish, stilted English, as well as his own language, and he shrugged and said, 'I do not mind where I am, so long as in time I have my own place to bring my Eva when we are to marry.'

'Don't worry about it.' Alex got to his feet, pushing the papers into his briefcase. 'I'll arrange something. You guys won't mind sharing a pad to begin with? Then you can take your time over set-tling in, look around for something more permanent.'

Imogen stood up too. Alex had called the meeting to a close and it had been a long day, discussing the future set-up at the new agency, breaking new ground over possible future campaigns, everything sparked off by yesterday's visit to the luxurious Devenko's Paris. She smiled at the others.

'I'll show you the area once the agency's off and running.' She tucked her black leather briefcase under her arm. 'I'm going to have to look for a place of my own; we can do the rounds together.'

'I'll hold you to that,' Pierre promised, his black eyes wicked. 'And if we find a place we both want, we won't fight over it. We'll do the civilised thing and share.'

'The possibility won't arise,' Alex stated curtly, and Imogen saw the looks of surprise Cathy and Stefan shot him, while Pierre simply leaned back in his chair, crossing his arms behind his head, his grin broad and mischievous. And Imogen frowned; for some reason Alex seemed to have a down on the Frenchman, which was odd, given that he had been singing his praises a few short weeks ago.

'We'll see you all at breakfast.' Alex slid a hand under Imogen's elbow and walked her to the door and, rather than show a split between very junior and definitely senior management, she bit back the objection that sprang to her tongue.

Dinner tonight would have been a chance to unwind and relax together after the stimulation of the past two days, to talk of ordinary, everyday things, to find out what made each other tick instead of endlessly discussing the new project.

And she had been looking forward to it because tomorrow, after breakfast, they would all be going their separate ways. She and Alex were booked on an early flight out of Charles de Gaulle, which wouldn't give much time for her to get to know her future colleagues on a more personal basis.

As the door closed behind them Alex bit out, 'For the sake of working relationships I'd prefer it if you didn't encourage Vinet.'

'I don't know what you mean.' Up until now he had been the perfect companion and colleague and she'd been able to put the darker side of his character right out of her mind. Trying to cover her disappointment, her voice had emerged on a snap and he countered acidly,

'Don't you? The man's been eyeing you for the last couple of days. He obviously felt confident enough to suggest you and he shack up together.'

'That was a joke,' she shot back coldly. She might have known the truce wouldn't last. And if she told him the truth, told him, 'I'm not that sort of girl,' he'd laugh in her face.

He already believed she'd been having an affair with Tolly, and he knew he could make her go mindless in his arms; so what more proof could he need to persuade him that she was open to an offer from Pierre Vinet?

She walked away from him, her high heels tapping on the cool marble floor, but before she gained the lift he was right beside her.

'Then it was in poor taste.'

He wasn't going to let the subject drop, she thought miserably, and he punched the lift button as if he were punching Pierre's head. 'In any case, the question of your house-hunting doesn't apply. You will be using the flat at Kynaston.'

Kynaston. His use of the house name made the whole project seem more real. And, from what she could remember of the flat above the stable block, it seemed perfect. But she knew, if he didn't, that Tolly had earmarked it for the staff Catrina would need to run the house for her once she and Alex were married.

But maybe Tolly hadn't really stressed that aspect—she didn't know, and she wasn't prepared to make an issue of it; so she entered the lift and stared straight ahead as he got in with her and said,

'I'll meet you in the bar in a couple of hours. We'll walk, find somewhere simple to eat. I'm tired of living in an hotel.'

She shrugged, said, 'OK.'

He said drily, 'Don't look so enthusiastic—I'd hate you to die of over-excitement.'

'I'd be more enthusiastic if I believed you wouldn't spend the entire evening lecturing me,' she answered stormily, still smarting over the way he had suggested that she would be only too eager to take up Pierre's joking offer. And he grinned lazily, his amber eyes crinkling at the corners.

'Oh, I won't. I can think of far more interesting things to do to you.'

Which sent a shivery sensation right down her spine, curling into her stomach, and, for her peace of mind, it presented possibilities that would be far more difficult to handle than any amount of lecturing.

He left her at the door to her room and she closed it behind her, leaning against it, closing her eyes. Alex Devenko, at his most insulting or his most seductive, was almost impossible to cope with.

She remembered the evening after Tolly had phoned to say goodbye; he'd said that Alex had been trying to get in touch with her, that he'd got something planned. The idea of seeing him again, so soon after she'd responded so instinctively to his lovemaking, had panicked her into taking herself off for a long walk, sitting in a cinema watching a film she couldn't even remember the title of, creeping back to her flat, putting out all the lights and taking the phone off the hook.

He'd phoned her the next morning at seven, waking her from a troubled sleep.

'Where the hell were you yesterday? Didn't Tolly tell you I'd been trying to contact you? I'd planned to take you out to dinner to discuss the details for the Paris trip.'

She'd had difficulty holding on to her temper because she'd known by then that the sexual interest he'd displayed in front of his father had been an act, that his decision to make love to her when he got her back home—to prise her away from the older man—had been abruptly shelved because she'd left him cold.

But she'd managed to keep her voice nice and even, if a little on the chilly side, when she'd replied, 'I'm sorry. I had too many things to do to waste time hanging around in case you might call. If you want to contact me in future, get your secretary to write a letter.'

Slamming the phone down had given her a lot of satisfaction. It wasn't the best way to start a new working relationship, but he'd had it coming to him. He'd insulted and threatened her, tried to blackmail her into walking away from the job, and from Tolly, had been reduced to trying to seduce her away from the older man, so yes, he'd had it coming.

She pushed herself away from the door and walked further into the elegant suite she'd been given. Spending the evening alone with Alex wasn't something she was looking forward to. When he was being pleasant, and there were other people around, she could cope with her confused feelings even though she was always stingingly aware of him.

Alone with him, deeply receptive to his every mood, how would she be able to handle the amalgam of resentment, unwilling sexual attraction and the plain and simple desire to slap his head off?

But she was going to have to try, she told herself firmly. She was now on Devenko's payroll, in the absence of Tolly Alex was her immediate boss, and they were going to have to get along together.

If he didn't bring up the unpleasant aspects of their earlier relationship, then neither would she. There was no point in opening up that particular can of worms again. She would try to behave as though they had met only a couple of days ago on the flight out from Gatwick. It was the only way to handle the situation that she could think of.

A long, lazy bath went some way towards relaxing her and as Alex had mentioned walking she dressed in a slate-grey fine wool skirt, a toning silk shirt, topped off with her white cashmere jacket. Black leather boots completed her outfit and, as she surveyed her reflection in the full-length, gilt-framed mirror, she chewed on her wide lower lip.

Without vanity, Imogen knew that she possessed the sophisticated beauty that gave the impression that she was very much a woman of the world, only the deep, pansy-dark eyes and generous mouth hinting at a warmth beneath the cool façade. Tonight she had deliberately used her make-up with a very light touch, pinned her silvery hair back in the French pleat she preferred when she was working, hoping to make herself look cool and remote. Prim.

At last, reasonably satisfied that her appearance belied the wriggles of half-terrified anticipation that were tormenting her at the thought of spending the evening with Alex, she left her room.

He was already in the bar, talking to the others. His beautifully tailored lovat suit set him apart almost as much as did his superlative looks. Cathy, Stefan and Pierre looked more like students in their casual jeans and baggy tops than the talented commercial artists they were, and they were laughing, chattering, winding down, and Imogen wished she could join them.

They were young, uncomplicated creatures, a world apart from the tricky, complex Alexsander Devenko, and she knew she could feel safe with them, unthreatened, while with Alex she never knew a moment's peace. She didn't trust him and, what was worse, she didn't trust herself.

Cathy was smiling up at him, hanging on his every word, but Alex turned as Imogen joined them, making her mouth stretch into a smile as Pierre flung a casual arm around her shoulders.

'I didn't think we'd be seeing you tonight. My luck must be in!'

'It just changed,' Alex said grimly, his brooding eyes on the Frenchman's hand as it lay lightly across Imogen's shoulder. And Imogen shuddered with angry reaction, but managed to extricate herself from Pierre's friendly embrace without betraying anything of what she was feeling as Alex placed a proprietorial hand on her arm, his fingers biting into her flesh like steel as he propelled her from the room.

He had no right to behave as if he owned her, but to object, in front of the others, would be a mistake. They weren't stupid and had already picked up on the brittle atmosphere between Alex and Vinet, and she would lose all credibility as their manager if she were to be seen brawling with the head of the company.

But as soon as they stepped outside the hotel she turned on him, her eyes sparkling with anger.

'I'm aware that you pay my wages. But out of working hours you don't own me!'

'Did I say I did?' he enquired coldly, his mouth a straight line, and she countered crossly,

'Not in so many words. But you act as though you do. Back there, for instance, did it ever occur to you that I might have preferred to spend the evening with the others?'

He took her arm, pulling her out of the way of a group of passers-by, hauling her against the hard length of his body, and his eyes narrowed, his mouth curling cynically as he riposted, 'I'm quite sure you would, and we both know why. You enjoy having Vinet make sheep's eyes at you.'

The man might be her boss but he was also insufferable and she didn't have to put up with his insults, or with the unwelcome body contact. Angrily, Imogen tried to pull away from him, but his arm immediately tightened around her waist, his attitude inexplicably changing as he told her,

'Forget it. Let's just enjoy the evening, hmm?'

He began to walk her over the paving stones, the lights from the buildings and streetlamps golden and hazy in the autumn mist, and she exhaled a long, pent-up breath and decided that making a scene, tearing a strip off him, was not an altogether wise thing to do.

Nevertheless, she wasn't backing down completely and she told him firmly, 'I'm willing to call a truce so long as you remember in future that out of working hours I'm a free agent. I can see who I please, do what I please.'

'I didn't hear that contentious comment,' he drawled, shortening his long stride to accommodate her shorter one. 'I refuse to spoil an evening in Paris with a beautiful woman with endless bickering,' and he pulled her by the hand towards a flower-seller, selected a long-stemmed white rose and handed it to her.

'It's not quite as lovely as you, but it's the nearest on offer.' His eyes were warm and his smile disarmed her, and her own lips twitched. It was impossible to stay angry with him when he smiled at her like that, and her stupid heart missed a beat as he dipped his head and brushed his lips lightly over hers.

Something would have to be done about the way he could make her react to him. She would either have to find a way to inject herself with a stiff dose of moral fibre, or tell him to lay off. A bit of both, she supposed.

Walking at his side through the streets, she felt the magic of Paris brush her like the wings of a moth, felt herself begin to relax. He was engaged to Catrina and he had made it plain that he believed her, Imogen, to be the worst kind of tramp, but she was going to allow herself to forget that, just for this one evening, and enjoy what this lovely city had to offer. Just one evening wouldn't hurt...

'They say Ernest Hemingway read his poetry aloud here.' Alex guided her gently through a group of street entertainers, colourful mime-artists and a very old organ-grinder. 'And that Sartre used to write here every morning.'

They entered the interior of the café, and Imogen blinked at the noise, the tobacco smoke. It was like something from a film set, walls of glittering mirrors, scarlet banquettes and brass-edged tables, waiters in crisp, floor-length aprons, the customers a variety show in themselves—old Frenchmen in navy berets inhaling Gitanes, ultra-thin women in stark black dresses, a young girl in a white lawn dress gazing adoringly into the eyes of a middle-aged man in a stiff business suit ... She drew in a great breath and Alex said,

'These sidewalk cafés are a good place to end the day. Parisians have turned the human penchant for doing nothing into an art form and enjoy nothing better than to come to such places, to drink a little, eat a little, talk, see and be seen. Let's enjoy, too.'

And she did. She couldn't remember when she'd taken so much pleasure in her surroundings, her companion. He was witty, attentive, utterly charming and, just for the evening, she allowed herself to fall in love a little.

It was only a little, and only for this one evening, she reminded herself as Alex ordered a vintage cognac with their *café noir*, turning to her, his golden eyes warm and alive in the handsome austerity of his authoritative features.

'Are you sure you won't try one of their sorbets? I believe they're out of this world.'

'I'd love to, but I'm stuffed!' she admitted inelegantly, and he grinned back at her.

'I know the feeling. Have a full meal here and you won't need to eat for a week.'

They'd started with a bowl of onion soup, thick melted cheese floating on the top with deliciously crisp croutons. Then fresh Belon oysters followed by thyme-flavoured roast lamb and a crisp salad with fragrant truffles. And the gutsy red wine they'd drunk with the meal must have been stronger than she'd realised because she couldn't seem to stop smiling, and her body felt boneless with unaccustomed languor. And she didn't even clam up when he asked,

'How come you're not married? I'd have thought a woman as lovely as you would have had to fight them off.'

She didn't even feel a prickle of warning and because, this evening, she'd found him so easy to talk to, she answered openly, 'I saw enough of my parents' marriage to put me off that state for life. I'd rather stick to my career; at least it doesn't jump up and snap my head off!' Or didn't, until she'd met up with Alexsander Devenko, she thought on a flicker of careless amusement.

And he asked, 'That bad, was it?' He was leaning back in his chair, his eyes half closed, watching her, swirling the brandy round in the glass, his eyes the exact colour of the potent liquid, and Imogen shrugged, pursing her lips and trying to look serious, privately amazed that her unhappy childhood really didn't seem to matter any more.

'They only married because I was on the way and they spent the rest of the time fighting each other. They only stayed together for my sake, but it would have been better if they'd split years before they did. One calm parent has got to be better than two yelling ones.'

'Do you see them?' he asked quietly, nodding to one of the waiters who came to refill the coffee-cups. And Imogen said,

'No. They're both remarried and have new families. Both live abroad, but we write sometimes. I don't think either of them would want to see me; at least, they've never suggested I visit. I'd only remind them of a time they'd rather forget.'

She drank some of the cognac and opened her eyes very wide as it slid down her throat. It made her feel very, very warm inside, almost melting, and she gave him a wide smile.

He remarked silkily, 'So you've written matrimony off as a non-starter, stick to your career and hand-pick your lovers.'

She knew he was referring to Tolly. Over the past couple of days, thank heavens, he had seen her in action with the plans she had laid out for setting up the new agency, must have seen for himself that she knew her job, could handle the team she would be working with. So he wouldn't be thinking Tolly had given her the position solely as a reward for her prowess in bed. But he obviously still believed she had her hooks in his father, was out for all she could get, she thought muzzily.

The idea of herself as a *femme fatale*, using her pillow-talk time with Tolly to wheedle as much out of him as she could, suddenly struck her as being ludicrous. Tolly was a dear, one of the nicest people she had ever known, but she could no more go to bed with him than fly. The whole scenario was screamingly funny and she began to giggle, sipping cognac recklessly.

Alex bit out, 'Stop that!'

He obviously didn't see the joke. She would like to explain it to him but he looked too ferocious. That seemed funny, too, and she snorted into her glass and would have drained it, but Alex took it out of her hand and pushed the cup of scalding hot coffee towards her.

'Drink that, then I'll take you back.'

She focused on him, her head on one side, saw the ice in his eyes, the tightening of his beautiful mouth, and nothing was funny any more.

He was back to being cross with her again, looking as though he loathed the sight of her, and that was sad because, up until now, they'd been having a wonderful time. He was the most spectacularly sexy man in the room and he'd had eyes only for her; he'd made her feel like a very special kind of princess.

Her big eyes filled with the sheen of tears. All she had done was giggle a little. Maybe she had giggled in the wrong place, but it wasn't such a crime, was it? And Alex groaned softly, got to his feet, fished a bundle of francs out of a pocket, dropped them on the table and came round to help her stand up.

'Can you walk, or shall I call a cab?' He draped her jacket round her shoulders, and he was too close to resist. Dropping her head against his broad chest, she snuggled closer to his warm male body and exhaled a long sigh of contentment.

'I can walk. I'm not drunk, you know. Just happy!'

'I'm glad to hear it,' he said drily, his fantastic mouth twitching at the corners, and her big eyes rested longingly on his lips. She wanted to kiss him more than anything else in the world!

But she wouldn't, of course she wouldn't. Involuntarily, she shook her head and primmed her mouth. She didn't go round kissing men whenever the fancy took her. Oh, no. Besides, he was going to marry some other girl. Catrina.

She began to thread her way through the tables, very carefully, planting her feet down solidly on the floor. She wondered if the poor sucker— Catrina, that was—knew that her fiancé flirted outrageously with other women, took them out on the town, plied them with strong drink. Or if she knew that he was quite prepared to make love to women just to seduce them away from his father!

That he hadn't been able to go through with it, because he had found the woman in question unfanciable, suddenly struck her as too depressing for words. She might just start to cry in a minute.

But Alex was right beside her as they hit the street, his arm supporting her, and she didn't want to cry any more. She felt deeply, gloriously happy, her feet floating over the pavement.

Paris was the most wonderful, romantic city in the world, and she was here, with the most sexy man in the world, and just for tonight she wasn't going to let herself even think of his low opinion of her. It would only spoil everything.

And there were stars in her eyes when they reached the door to her suite. The upstairs corridors were hushed, very luxurious, and she wondered if he would end the evening in the time-honoured tradition and kiss her.

Of their own accord, her lips parted in anticipation, but he had taken the key from her fingers and was opening the door, and he said wryly, 'I should have kept a closer eye on your alcohol intake. I keep forgetting you're not as sophisticated as you look.'

Which wasn't exactly a romantic thing to say, she thought, following him into the room, her lips pouting, tripping over her feet.

Quickly, his arm came out to steady her, and she sagged against him, winding her arms around his waist, beneath the open jacket of his suit. And the contact was delicious.

Her breathing went haywire. And she knew he'd been affected, too, because she heard the sudden intake of his breath and she lifted her head, her throat arching, her eyes going smoky as they fastened on the utterly, devastatingly sensual line of his mouth.

But he pushed her gently away from him, a frown-line between his eyes, and he said curtly, 'Sit down, before you fall.'

So she did, sinking on to a brocade-covered chair at the side of the bed, her eyes puzzled. And he knelt in front of her, tugging off her boots, then hauled her to her feet again and began undressing her as if she were a doll.

Imogen tried to help him, but she felt so weak with longing that her efforts were worse than useless, so she gave up the attempt.

She gazed at the severity of his breathtaking features as he unbuttoned her silk shirt, exposing her taut breasts as they strained against the filmy barrier of her tiny lacy bra, and her bones turned to water. Earlier, she had thought she was falling in love, just a little. Now she knew she had gone the whole way, fallen in love completely.

She tried to wind her arms around his neck, to find the words to tell him how she felt, but the shock of the revelation had been too much for her and she felt her knees give way completely.

Muttering under his breath, Alex scooped her up and dropped her on the bed, making the breath come out of her lungs in a whoosh. But her eyes opened very wide as he continued to strip her, his golden eyes grim.

He was going to make love to her, she thought hazily, her heart beginning to pound against her ribs, a melting languor invading her entire body at the prospect of the inevitable conclusion to the magical evening when she'd discovered she'd fallen in love for the very first time.

But, when every last scrap of lacy underwear had been removed, he straightened, pulling the light feather duvet over her body, right up to her chin.

'Alex?' She wriggled her arms out from under the covering, holding them up to him, a slight frown drawing her fine brows together. And he bent quickly, touching her parted lips lightly with his own, shaking his dark head.

'Not tonight, sweetheart. I like my women sober.' He walked to the door, his back rigid, but there was a gentleness in his tone that made her want to weep as, just before closing the door behind him, he told her, 'Sleep, pet. You won't remember a thing in the morning, I promise.'

CHAPTER SIX

But Imogen did. She remembered every last shaming detail. She didn't think she would ever be able to forget what had happened, the way the unaccustomed intake of alcohol had made every last one of her inhibitions fly out of the window, the way she had practically thrown herself at Alexsander's head.

She was standing outside the terminal building at Gatwick, waiting for Alex to bring the car round, her spine rigid, her face pale in the thin late-autumn sunshine. During the drive back into London she could hardly maintain the polite silence she'd managed on the flight over, pretending to be engrossed in the notes she'd made over the last two days.

She was dreading the coming enforced intimacy, knowing that her behaviour of the night before could only have reinforced his scabrous opinion of her. Her stomach churned sickeningly. How could she have acted that way? Even to the extent of believing herself in love with the brute! She was no such thing. She had more sense.

The Jaguar slid up in front of her and Alex got out, sparing her a brief, quizzical look before taking their luggage and stowing it in the boot. Quickly, she got into the passenger-seat and tried to compose herself, willing the flutters of apprehension and self-disgust to die down.

Not by a word or a look had he so far given any indication that he recalled her wanton behaviour of the night before—the way he had stripped her naked without a single protest coming from her. Indeed, she'd been positively encouraging him!

She tried to push that thought out of her mind but it wouldn't go. And her face was scarlet when he slid in beside her, and she tried to concentrate on his light, uncontroversial conversation as he drove out of the airport environs; but all she could think of was the way she had woken that morning, stark naked, the memories of the night before making her writhe with embarrassment.

Her head had been hammering unbearably and, although she hadn't been able to face breakfast, not even a cup of coffee, she had joined the others, blaming her lack of appetite on an entirely fictitious fear of flying, doing her best to keep up with the quick-fire conversation and trying to avoid looking in Alex's direction because she knew if she met his eyes she would turn a brilliant shade of scarlet.

And when Cathy had said, 'I'm not flying back until this evening. It would be criminal to come to Paris and not do some shopping. I was thinking of going to Andrea Pfister on Rue Cambon. I've heard they have the most gorgeous shoes—at not-bad prices, either. Why don't you see if you can swap your flight ticket, Imogen? We could have a great time looking at all the fantastic things we can't afford to buy!' Imogen had been very tempted.

Not that she relished the thought of window-shopping, even in Paris, but spending the day here would mean she didn't have to catch the earlier flight and endure Alex's company.

'Do that,' Pierre had put in. 'Stefan has a midday flight back to Munich, but I could meet up with you girls, give you lunch and show you something of my city.'

But Alex had interrupted coldly, 'Imogen has too much to do to waste time trotting around Paris. The agency has to be fully functional by the new year, and she's being paid to see that it happens.'

Ordinarily, Imogen would have been incensed by his arbitrary stick-waving. Even if he was the boss and fully entitled to do so, he could have been a darn sight more tactful about it. But she'd felt too wrecked, both physically and mentally, to do anything more than give Cathy and Pierre an apologetic smile and murmur, 'Some other time, maybe.'

And now Alex asked, 'Headache better?' and she swallowed convulsively. This was the first reference he'd made to her stupid behaviour of the night before and she knew she had to apologise.

When walking away from her wanton presence, he'd told her she would have forgotten all about it when she woke. Well, she hadn't. He'd been wrong.

But he wasn't to know that. If she could pretend she'd forgotten everything except the disgraceful fact that she'd had too much to drink, she wouldn't need to cringe too badly whenever they encountered each other in the future.

So she ran her tongue over her dry lips and managed, throatily, 'I'm sorry about what happened, about having too much to drink, I mean. I don't make a habit of getting legless—I'm just not used to it.'

And he grinned crookedly. 'I know that, now. And if all you have to feel sorry about is a glass of wine too many, then you don't really have to worry, do you?'

He was prodding, she knew he was, trying to gauge if she recalled what had happened later. And she was going to ignore it, act dumb, so she stared ahead through the windscreen, horribly aware of the amused glance he darted in her direction, and felt her face turn fiery-red.

So that was a dead give-away, wasn't it? And she bit her lip, hating herself, but hating him even more.

Staring out of the window at her side, she couldn't think of a single thing to say to break the thick silence. It was oppressing her, making her want to scream. She knew he was laughing at her inside his head, recalling the foolish spectacle she'd made of herself, cynically deciding that his former opinion of her morals hadn't been set nearly low enough!

Wallowing in the misery of her thoughts, she came back to reality with a jerk, realising he'd pulled the car up and was getting out. They were on the outskirts of Windsor and she said, stupidly, 'This isn't Shepherd's Bush,' because she'd taken it for granted he was driving her home.

'No. At least it wasn't the last time I looked at a map,' he responded, poker-faced. 'There are one or two things I need. Won't be a moment.'

She watched as he disappeared into a small general store and when he came out he was carrying a bulging cardboard box.

She said, 'What are we doing here?'

'I thought we'd take a look at Kynaston,' he told her, sliding into the seat beside her and starting the engine. 'The decorators should be finished by now and you might like to take a more detailed look at the flat. You've only been out the once, haven't you?'

She nodded. She'd been looking forward to getting back to the privacy of her own place, out of his disturbing company. She needed to be quite alone to come to terms with her own embarrassment and self-disgust.

But he had a point; visiting the flat she would be moving into in a couple of weeks' time was a reasonable idea. She would be able to judge what she'd need in the way of extra furnishings. The Shepherd's Bush flat was too tiny to accommodate anything beyond the basic essentials.

'You don't mind, do you? Or do you have a date for this evening you don't want to break?' There was an edge of what sounded like irritation in his voice and she shrugged,

'I don't seem to have much choice, do I?' and stared sullenly ahead as they left the streets of Windsor behind with a growl of the engine that seemed to echo his mood. She wasn't about to pretend an exhilaration she wasn't feeling. Looking over the flat was a good idea, but being on her own, in the privacy of her own space, away from him, was an even better one!

At Kynaston he parked the Jaguar in the courtyard which was bounded by the stable block and the outbuildings which were being converted for the agency's use, and she could hear the sound of hammering, someone whistling the latest pop hit, as the huge rooms were being partitioned into separate offices and studios.

Alex handed her a key. 'Look round the flat while I see how the builders are getting on; they should finish by the end of the week. If they don't I'll want to know the reason why. I've arranged for the decorators to start on Monday, and I don't want them to be kept hanging around.'

He strode away from her and Imogen shivered. The early-November sun was a hazy red disc low in the sky and the air was chilly. But the involuntary *frisson* had more to do with Alex than the ambient temperature. He was a formidable character, and heaven help those who didn't live up to his high standards! If the cheerfully whistling builders were running behind schedule, she pitied them!

Clutching the key, she walked carefully up the stone steps that clung to the outside of the stable block. Her legs felt decidedly shaky. She hadn't been able to face eating all day but now her stomach was protesting, lack of food making her feel light-headed.

The slight dizziness passed as she slotted the key in the lock and walked into a narrow hallway. Several doors led off and she opened them all. The flat was far larger than the one she would be leaving, with two bedrooms, sitting-room, bathroom and kitchen. She would enjoy living in more spacious surroundings.

The click of her booted heels echoed on the bare boards and she rubbed a clear space on the grimy glass of one of the sitting-room windows, looking down on to the courtyard, and Alex said, right behind her,

'There's quite a lot to be done before you can move in here.'

Imogen jumped round, her heart in her mouth.

'Do you have to creep up on people? I nearly died of fright!'

He grinned, his golden eyes alight as he gently flicked the end of her nose with a forefinger.

'I perfected the strategy years ago. Creep up on a beautiful woman and shout ''Boo'' in her ears and she ends up quivering in my arms!'

'Not this one!' she muttered stormily, removing herself to the other side of the room, opening one of the built-in cupboards at the side of the hearth recess and peering in.

And he was right behind her, his beautiful voice low and warm as he told her, 'Then I shall have to re-think my tactics, shan't I?' and he placed his hand lightly on her shoulders, easing her back against the hard length of his body, making her go rigid as she fought to control her instinctive and utterly alarming reaction to him.

He only had to touch her to set her pulses singing; it was an immutable equation based on sexual chemistry, an unwelcome fact of life. Something she had to get to grips with and control.

He was flirting with her again. Still trying to use his considerable male sexuality to seduce her away from his father? Didn't he realise she knew what a sham it all was? She wasn't a complete fool and had long since worked out why his attitude had changed from one of threatening insults to sexual invitation. And she was only too painfully aware that, physically, she left him cold.

She had had two humiliating proofs of that! Twice he had reduced her to a mass of mindless needs, and twice he had walked away, unable to force himself to take what was on offer.

Shuddering, she banged the cupboard door shut and twisted away from him, and he asked, 'Seen enough? We'll go up to the house. It's too damn cold to hang around here longer than we have to.'

She had no choice, of course. Swallowing her impatience, she followed him outside and managed to keep up with the brisk pace he set as they walked beneath the skeletal trees and across the lawns to the big house.

Simply being with him set her nerves on edge. He had taught her things about herself she would rather not have known. She longed, quite desperately, to be on her own, back in the privacy of her own little flat where she could make herself a scratch meal and curl up in her warm bed with an engrossing book and try to forget the embarrassment of the last twenty-four hours.

A thin grey dusk was falling, the air decidedly cold as Alex opened the main door, flicking a switch so that the hall was flooded with light. And he walked ahead of her, opening doors to all the

ground-floor rooms, and everywhere was newly
decorated, fully and elegantly furnished, fitted
carpets underfoot, the warmth of the central heating
curling into her bones, making Imogen relax despite herself.

'I don't believe it,' she said, her violet eyes wide.
'The last time I was here the place was empty—all
bare boards and echoing rooms.'

'That was four, five weeks ago,' he smiled
smugly. 'It's surprising what one can achieve in that
time, if you know who to bark your orders at.
Come on, let's see if everything's as it should be
upstairs.'

It was. Needless to say, instructions had been
followed to the letter, and it helped, of course,
Imogen decided tartly, if one had the financial clout
to back up the orders he had talked about.

Preceding him into one of the bedroom suites,
luxuriously decorated and furnished in shades of
soft yellow and off-white, she stated, 'I admire
Tolly's taste. Everything's perfect, but not osten-
tatiously so.'

'Tolly had nothing to do with it.' Alex was leaning
back against the polished mahogany door, his hands
thrust into the pockets of his trousers, totally relaxed. 'He's been in the States for the past four
weeks, remember?'

So he had. Imogen went over to inspect the delicate dressing-table, complete with cut-crystal pots
and jars, trying to appear engrossed. Tolly had
bought the house, but had left the choice of furnishings to his son. And that made sense, because
Kynaston would belong to Alex and Catrina when

they married. And for some reason—a reason she was highly reluctant to look into—she suddenly felt utterly depressed.

'The bathroom's through there.' Alex dipped his dark head in the direction of a second door. 'I expect you'd like to freshen up after the journey. There's something I need to fetch from the car; I'll be in the kitchen when you're ready.'

She watched him go through her long, dark lashes, her head bent. She wished she'd never met him. He made her feel things she didn't want to feel. And knowing he believed her to be a tramp, her motives murky, made everything so much worse. And knowing that one day, probably quite soon, he would be marrying Catrina and living with her in this beautiful house didn't help at all.

Since meeting him her emotions had run riot. It was the first time since early childhood that she had allowed that to happen. As a child she had learned that emotions could hurt if they were allowed to get out of hand.

So she was going to have to get back into control, wasn't she?

Squaring her shoulders, she walked into the bathroom, fern-green and crisp white, stripped off her suit-jacket and rolled up the sleeves of her blouse.

Alex Devenko affected her as no other man ever had before, and that was a fact she was going to have to live with. No doubt, in time, his effect on her would die the death and she would be able to look back on this period in her life with amused detachment.

All she had to do was remind herself that he belonged to another woman. Even if he didn't, it would make no difference, because he wouldn't have her if she came gift-wrapped. The way he'd walked away from her last night, when she'd tipsily as good as begged him to make love to her, was ample proof of that!

Ten minutes later she felt much better, calmer, fresher. Carrying her jacket over her arm, she found her way back down to the kitchen. If he ever laid a hand on her again she would tell him, loudly and clearly, that he didn't have to sacrifice himself to keep his father out of the clutches of a cheap little gold-digger. There was, quite simply, nothing to save his father from.

No doubt it would come as a huge relief to him— in more ways than one!

He had plugged in the filter machine and the tantalising aroma of fresh coffee made her nostrils twitch appreciatively. Glancing at her, his golden eyes warm, he invited, 'Sit down. Coffee won't be long, and I expect you're hungry; I know I am.'

He was unpacking the contents of the box he'd carried out of the general store, his capable, long-fingered hands deft as he unwrapped cheeses, bread and salad stuffs. Those beautifully made hands had been just as deft as they'd undressed her last night, those long fingers brushing intimately against her flesh——

She jerked her head round quickly, her cheeks burning as she tried to shut out the unwelcome thoughts that persisted in invading her mind.

'Nice kitchen,' she commented politely, steeling herself to ignore the poise-threatening tension that was making her muscles feel rigid. 'Shall I wash the salad?'

'I'll do it.' He carried lettuce, tomatoes and celery over to the stainless-steel double sink. 'I need to find out where everything's kept because, from tomorrow, I'll be moving in here.' A gush of cold water punctuated his words and he reached up to pine wall-cupboards, searching for bowls. 'I'm sick of living in hotels and I'll be on hand to keep an eye on the alterations in progress.'

There was nothing Imogen could say to that; his decision made pretty good sense and, in any case, it was nothing to do with her. Had he been anyone else she would have been able to keep up a sensible, interested conversation, but his mere presence addled her brain, turned her into a different woman.

And he, she recognised sickly, was aware of it. The slight, satisfied smile on his sexy mouth, as he moved relaxedly around the large, warm room, pulling the burnt-orange linen curtains to shut out the grey November darkness outside, bringing plates and cutlery to the central pine table, sent shivers of mortified apprehension down her spine.

He knew exactly how he affected her and the knowledge amused him, probably gave him a feeling of power. The monster was clearly enjoying himself at her expense and the more withdrawn and tense she got the more he would gloat. And she wouldn't give him the satisfaction.

Stiffening her spine, Imogen gave him a thin smile as he put the salad bowl down by the cheese and bread and brought the coffee-jug over. She wouldn't let him get to her. As far as she was concerned, last night had never happened, and the sooner he understood that the better.

From now on their relationship would be conducted on a purely business level and she helped herself to milk, stirred it into the dark, hot brew and stated coolly, 'I have to be out of my flat in two weeks' time. I take it I can move straight in over the old stables?' There shouldn't be any difficulty; she could do the necessary painting after she'd moved her few possessions in, and she'd only brought the subject up to show him he couldn't reduce her to a state of tongue-tied mortification, that her behaviour of last night was the last thing on her mind.

But he sat down opposite her, cutting a chunk off the granary loaf, holding it out to her on the point of the knife, his face bland as he told her, 'Out of the question. The place won't be fit to live in for at least a couple of months. There are damp patches on some of the ceilings that suggest the roof is in urgent need of repair and the wiring is positively dangerous. I'll arrange for a surveyor to give it the once-over and make recommendations. But, as I said before, you'll be looking at a time-span of at least a couple of months before you can even think of moving in. Cheese?'

Imogen stared at him, her mouth tightening, her eyes furious. It had been Alex himself who had suggested she use the flat in the first instance, intimating that it would be far more convenient for her to be on the spot to finalise the detailed work of setting up the agency. And now, when he knew she had given notice to her landlord, had to be out of her flat within two weeks, he was telling her she would have nowhere to go!

'It's not going to create problems, I hope?' he asked suavely, lavishly buttering his bread. He knew his unwelcome news would create a whole bundle of them and she hated him for his air of bland insouciance, wanted to scream at him that he knew damned well it would.

But never again would she allow him to make her lose her control over her emotions, so she pinned a sugary smile to her face and told him, 'None that I can't solve,' and began to force herself to eat the food on her plate because to push it aside, as she wanted to do, would only give him the satisfaction of knowing he had ruined her appetite.

How she was going to find accommodation within easy reach of Windsor, in her price bracket, within two short weeks, when her earlier enquiries had assured her that such places were as rare as icicles in the Sahara, she didn't know; and when he said,

'If you do run into difficulties, let me know,' she couldn't stop the rash reply.

'And what will you do? Wave a magic wand?'

'If you ask me to.' His grin was disarming but she wasn't in the mood to be disarmed. She felt sick with annoyance and the cheese was sticking in her throat. Every time she had anything to do with

him he caused problems, so the only sensible thing
to do was keep out of his way as much as possible.

She looked quickly at her watch and manufac-
tured an expression of surprise.

'Heavens! I'd no idea it was this time; I have to
get back.' She stood up, forcing a smile. 'But stay
where you are, I can phone for a taxi.' She couldn't
bear to be in his company a moment longer, she
couldn't endure the way he made her feel, as if she
had no control over her emotions. He either made
her want to kiss him, or kick him, putting her equilibrium into a state of chaos.

'Important date, is it?' Alex asked, lines of cyni-
cism bracketing his sensual mouth. 'Does Tolly
know just how much you put it around whenever
his back's turned?'

Imogen shot him a hating stare, her face going
crimson. If she denied his supposition of a date she
would be defeating the object of the exercise, the
need to remove herself from his disturbing company
at once. And if she denied his crude accusation he
would laugh in her face. He had been there, hadn't
he, when she'd as good as offered herself to him
last night?

So she said nothing, feeling her anger and outrage
churn around impotently inside her, making her
shake as she walked over to the wall-mounted tele-
phone near one of the huge pine dressers.

But as she lifted the handset his fingers tightened
cruelly around her wrist and she gasped in shock
and pain. He had moved so quietly and quickly,
taking her by surprise, and his voice bit into her
ear,

'I brought you out here, I'll take you back. And who knows? I might just hang around long enough to give the poor sucker a word of warning.'

He took the handset from her nerveless fingers, his face hard as he told her with cold authority, 'Put the foodstuff in the fridge while I bring the car up to the house.'

His grip on her wrist had loosened and Imogen dragged her hand away, her eyes dark with unspoken mutiny as she rubbed the reddened skin. He was breathing as rapidly as she and she backed away, the anger she felt in him an almost tangible violence.

She saw his mouth tighten before he swung round and walked from the room and she shuddered with reaction as she hurriedly began pushing the food into the fridge.

Knowing what he believed her relationship with his father to be, she would have thought he would have been over the moon with relief if he believed her to be seeing another man in Tolly's absence. It would be, to his way of thinking, another piece of evidence to place before his misguided parent, damning her as a tramp in the eyes of the wealthy, elderly man who was supposed to be her lover.

But instead of looking triumphant he had been searingly angry. She couldn't understand him.

And he would be back in a matter of minutes. It would take very little time to bring the Jaguar round from where he had left it in the old stable-yard, and she would have her jacket on, be waiting for him in the hall, calm and composed, never letting him see how much his vile insults could hurt her.

But he was back before she had time to dump the used plates and mugs in the sink, let alone get herself into her suit-jacket, get herself some semblance of composure.

He was in the door aperture, his attitude almost one of indolence, and the triumph that had been missing before, its absence puzzling her, was unmistakably there as he told her, 'We'll neither of us be going anywhere tonight. You can't see a hand in front of your face out there, so you might as well get used to the idea of spending the night with me.'

CHAPTER SEVEN

'I'M NOT staying here,' Imogen stated tersely. She didn't trust Alex. He could flay her alive with his cruel tongue and she already felt too raw to endure any more of his stinging company. All she craved was the privacy and peace of her own little home, a chance to lick her wounds.

'You have no alternative,' he responded easily, meeting her stormy eyes with a slow, bland smile. 'See for yourself.'

He moved aside, making a lazy, 'after-you' gesture with one hand and she darted him a quick, mistrusting look and stalked out of the room, down the flagged corridor and into the huge hall.

And he was right beside her as she tugged the heavy front door open, his golden eyes mocking as he watched the shock hit her face.

Thick, dark-grey fog hung like a heavy blanket, shrouding everything, the light from the open doorway scarcely penetrating at all. It was very quiet and very cold and she could hear her own ragged breathing, and before she could give way to the panic she felt building up inside her she said stonily, 'I can understand your not wanting to risk the Jag. I'll phone for a taxi,' and felt her hackles rise as he gave a low, amused chuckle.

'If you can find a driver willing to make the return journey in this lot, I'll personally walk in front of you with a red flag!'

He was right, of course, and admitting it didn't make her feel one bit better.

She snapped childishly, 'It's all your fault!' and shivered convulsively.

'If you think I can call down a pea-souper, just for the dubious pleasure of keeping you here, then you've got rocks in your head,' he retorted impatiently, pulling her against his side with one determined hand, reaching for the heavy door with the other and slamming it, shutting out the cold, damp fog.

'I could have been home hours ago if you hadn't insisted on coming out here,' Imogen protested, her voice muffled against the solid wall of his chest. He, too, had discarded his suit-jacket, and the shocking impact of his body heat, through the fine cotton of his shirt, made her gasp.

The temptation to stay exactly where she was, to press herself closer to Alex's hard, warm masculine body, was strong. But she resisted it, pressing both hands against his chest to push herself away, but he hauled her back, using both hands now to subdue her, his fingers biting into her shoulders as he grated back at her, his tone barbed, 'And all wrapped up, snug and cosy, with your date-of-the-day! Sorry, precious, but you're just going to have to make do with me.'

She shuddered beneath the icy hostility of his eyes and shook her head miserably. His opinion of her couldn't be lower and that mattered to her, mat-

tered on a deep and personal level that she was reluctant to understand. She needed his respect, his
liking, needed it with a desperation that was totally
new to her.

But how to convince him that his opinion of her
was misguided, a complete figment of his own over-
coloured imagination? His belief in her lack of
morals was too deeply entrenched to be easily wiped
out.

And suddenly the task seemed beyond her; the
closeness of his warm, devastatingly male body, the
way his hands had gentled and were now softly
kneading the slender bones of her shoulders had
weakened her, sapped her strength, and she dragged
her tongue over her parched lower lip, trying to
formulate the words that would make him understand how wrong he was about her. But the words
wouldn't come and she felt her body curve weakly
into his and heard his small, audible intake of
breath as his body tensed to take the weight of hers,
heard him say, his voice harsh with bitter self-
mockery,

'And don't think the idea doesn't tempt me. But
I'm choosy about my sleeping partners.'

The insult got through to her, setting a quick burn
of rage running through her veins, giving her the
strength to drag herself together. And she flung her
head back, her eyes brilliant with anger as she bit
out, 'I'm not like that—you assume too damned
much!'

'Any assumptions I make are based on solid fact.'
His mouth curved cynically as he released his grip
on her and pushed her away. 'And, if your re-

lationship with Tolly, your encouragement of Vinet and the date you were painfully reluctant to break this evening weren't enough, I have the evidence of last night to go on. You were practically begging for it.' He gave her a hard, glittering look before swinging away, walking back to the kitchen, and Imogen sagged back against the closed door, pushing her knuckles against her teeth.

Trying to make him believe she was not the callous wanton of his imagination would be like trying to knock a brick wall down with her head. Painful and futile. Weeks ago, with Tolly's help, she would have been able to convince him. But not now. As far as Alex was concerned she had dug her own grave and jumped into it, and she silently cursed the unwilling attraction that had led her to make those tipsy advances to him.

Trouble was, she reflected miserably as she levered herself away from the door, despite his scathing opinion of her, his calculated insults, the attraction was growing stronger. Physical desires were contrary monsters at the best of times, feeding on a look, a single smile, a turn of the head, an inflexion of a voice. Feeding, growing bigger, stronger...

Imogen pulled her breath in through her nostrils and closed her eyes, counting to ten very slowly. She had to win back her composure, face him, face the contempt in his eyes. Running out into the blanketing fog would get her precisely nowhere except spread-eagled against the first tree she blundered into.

Steeling herself, she followed him to the kitchen where he was clattering dishes in the sink, the hot water gushing from the tap. Swallowing hard, she pitched her voice to carry over the noise he was making and requested, 'May I have your car keys, please?' and watched him go very still.

And then he swung round, his hands dripping suds, his short bark of laughter holding no amusement at all as he scorned, 'If you imagine I'm going to let you drive my car——'

'I'm not that crazy,' she cut in coldly. 'Why can't you begin to think straight for a change? I merely want to bring my case in from the boot,' and had the satisfaction of seeing him look abashed. And then the shutters were down again, his heart-stopping features blank as he reached for a towel and roughly dried his hands.

'I'll get them. Put more coffee on, would you? I've got the feeling this is going to be one of the longest, toughest evenings of my life.'

Quite what he meant by that she couldn't fathom, and she wasn't going to waste time in trying because, for her part, she would be taking herself off to bed the moment he brought in her things. He could have a long, tough evening all by himself!

Working quickly, she washed the remaining dishes and stacked them on the stainless-steel drainer, hunting around for where the coffee was kept and spooning it haphazardly into the filter machine. She was sick of fighting with Alex, sick of his bewildering mood-changes, sick of herself for the way she was beginning to feel about him.

And how did she feel about him? she asked herself drearily, and didn't have time to answer herself because she heard the front door bang, heard his decisive footsteps as he approached along the corridor.

Deliberately, she made her face blank as she turned when he walked through the door, putting both cases down on the floor. And she said, 'Thank you,' very politely and moved towards him, picking up her own case, holding it defensively in front of her as she asked, not looking at him, fixing her big violet eyes at some point beyond his left shoulder, 'I'd like to go to bed, if you'll tell me which room you'd like me to use.'

'Running away so soon?' There was something underneath the slow drawl she couldn't put a name to and she refused to be drawn into a battle of words yet again. Today had already seemed longer than any day had a right to be so she clamped her lips together, tightened her grip on her case, and he said tersely, 'And as for which room I'd like you to use— how would you react if I said mine?'

The intentness of his tone, more than the words he'd used, jolted her out of her assumed indifference and her eyes flew to his, a slight frown drawing her brows together as she saw the brooding heat in his stare as it moved with lazy assessment over her body.

The shirt she was wearing was a slate-grey silk, thin and fine, and she knew the lacy black bra she wore beneath it would show through as a seductive shadow, her pale skin a beckoning glimmer. And as his eyes rested with open appreciation on the twin peaks she felt them harden, pushing against the restricting fabric, and knew, with a shame that burned over her face, that he was very well aware of what was happening to her.

She wanted to turn and run but her feet were rooted to the ground and her heart began thudding crazily against her breastbone.

Her skin began to prickle with sensual reaction, as if his hands were touching her, and the silence between them was thick, loud with unspoken desires, and there were only the two of them here, bound by this brittle awareness, only the two of them in a fog-wrapped world, and the case she had been holding so defensively slipped from her nerveless fingers and the sound of the thud as it hit the quarry tiles broke the spell and his features were wiped clean, his mouth compressing into a hard line of distaste as he turned.

He bit out, 'Use the yellow room. You rather liked it, as I recall.'

And if he'd meant to say goodnight she didn't stay long enough to find out as, with thudding heartbeats, she took the stairs at an undignified run, hauling her suitcase with her.

The room she'd been in earlier was easy enough to find and there was a lock on the door, and only when she'd turned the key did she allow herself to relax, reaction setting in, making her shake.

The effect Alex had on her was catastrophic; he only had to look at her in that certain way to make her want him. Since she had met him he had turned her safe theory of emotional detachment right round on its head.

And she knew, with a certainty that made her blood run cold, that she could fall in love with him, and that it would be for keeps.

But she wasn't going to let that happen, was she?

Her face set, she marched over to the bed and pulled down the pretty yellow coverlet. Thankfully, it was made up; the interior designers Alex had employed had done their job to perfection and she wouldn't have to go searching for bed linen and run the risk of bumping into him again tonight. She simply wasn't up to another encounter.

A long soak in the adjoining bathroom went some way towards relaxing her and, selecting a nightdress out of her case, she slipped it on and sat in front of the mirror, pulling a brush through her long silvery hair.

There were a lot of things she had to sort out— the setting up of the agency, finding somewhere to live once her time at the Shepherd's Bush flat ran out, not to mention the knotty problem of her troubled relationship with Alex, her own perverse reaction to him.

They were going to have to work together and somehow she would have to make herself immune to his particularly devastating brand of sexuality. Somehow. To allow the feelings she had for him to grow would be asking for trouble. He disliked and distrusted her and he was engaged to marry another woman. And that alone was ample reason to knock some sense into her stupid head.

But, as she had known since childhood, sense and proportion evaporated on the searing breath of uncontrolled emotion!

*   *   *

Surprisingly, she slept well, waking to clear skies, only a slight drifting of mist to soften the stark outlines of the skeletal trees. A clear mind, too.

Climbing out of bed, she knew exactly what she had to say to Alex; the right approach was the only thing she had to work out.

Padding over the luxuriously soft off-white carpet, she routed in her suitcase and pulled out the casual trousers and matching top she'd taken to Paris but hadn't found the occasion to wear. Fortunately, the crêpy wool fabric didn't crease and the clear peacock-blue colour suited her, making her eyes look even darker than usual, her skin softer and paler.

She looked casual but in control, she decided as she caught her long silky hair back at the nape of her neck, and that was exactly the approach she would use.

If she was to fight the effect Alex had on her, fight her own body's treacherous response to him, then she would need all the weapons she could lay her hands on. Coolness, her ability to think clearly and logically, were contents of her armoury she couldn't afford to mislay.

She'd made toast and the coffee was ready by the time he came down and joined her in the kitchen. He looked fresh and vital, newly shaved, his dark hair still damp from the shower. And her stupid heart missed a beat, reacting to his sheer physical magnificence, but she quelled the unwanted flutterings with gritty mental determination and gave him a cool smile.

'I'm glad to see the fog's lifted,' she remarked levelly as she poured the coffee and ignored the puzzled glance he gave her. 'The toast's ready and, while we eat, I suggest we talk, rationally and calmly.'

She sat down, reaching for a slice of hot toast and buttering it, her head bent. But she didn't miss they way one of his dark eyebrows curved up, his amber gaze slightly amused as he joined her at the table. And she ignored that, too, as best she could, giving her undivided attention to the small task of slicing her toast into neat segments.

Annoyingly, her pulse-beat had quickened, and his presence, the amused yet intent way he was watching her, was directly responsible for that. And when he drawled, 'So, what's the subject of the rational talk we're going to have?' she dropped her knife with a tiny clatter, stinging sensation creeping down her backbone. That deep, sexy voice of his could always get to her; it was a seduction in itself.

But she controlled herself quickly, pulling her skittering senses together, and told him firmly, 'Our relationship.'

'I see,' he said slowly. 'What about it? If it calls for discussion, then that means, *per se*, that a change is needed.' He was leaning back in his chair, one arm hooked over the back-rest, seemingly totally relaxed. But his eyes were very intent, an indication that he wasn't entirely immune to the tension between them, and Imogen found her own eyes held, only dropping to his engagingly sensual mouth as it curved slightly upwards and he asked softly, 'What kind of change did you have in mind?'

His gaze held hers with an intimate intensity that sent a wave of turbulence churning through her. She knew, only too well, the nature of the change he was suggesting, knew he was waiting for her to take it up and give him one more massive piece of evidence to put before his father.

Carefully biting into a piece of toast, Imogen hid a small, bitter smile. She knew what he was up to, knew the way his devious mind worked. And boy, was he in for a disappointment!

Swallowing, she lobbed a cool smile in his direction and stated decisively, 'For the sake of our professional relationship we have to learn to live with each other,' and elicited a low chuckle from him. Leaning forward to pour them both more coffee, he smiled into her eyes.

'Literally, or figuratively?' His smile was mockingly devastating and, for a moment, she stared at him, her lips parted, before she was able to pull herself together with a little shake of her head.

'Figuratively, of course.'

'You disappoint me.' But there was no regret in those dancing golden eyes, just lazy enjoyment of the way he was taking a rise out of her. And she took a few sips of coffee to give herself time to fight back the impulse to hit his head. Controlled yet casual, that was the way to play it, she reminded herself briskly. Uninvolved, unemotional...

'I'm trying to tell you that, for the sake of our working relationship, we have to put the past few weeks behind us,' she told him calmly, resisting the impulse to rub her hands down the side of her trousers to rid her palms of the slick of sweat that was gathering there.

She never felt uninvolved or unemotional in his company, and that was what she was fighting. And the only way to fight the mess he made of her emotions was to batten them down, push them out of sight and pretend they didn't exist.

So, to that end, she ploughed doggedly on.

'We've had our disagreements,' she understated deliberately. There was no point in stirring up murky waters again, was there—not if they were going to establish a calmer relationship? 'The rights or wrongs of which I see no need to go into. I simply suggest that we put them behind us, begin again, keeping our dealings with each other entirely professional and, hopefully, friendly. Otherwise, I don't see how we are going to manage to work together.'

'Entirely logical,' Alex agreed, a suspicious twitch at one corner of his mouth drawing a faint, condemnatory line between her eyes. 'However, as for our working together, we're going to have to manage that, come what may. And friendly?' His mouth straightened. 'I don't think we'll ever manage that, do you?'

He stood up suddenly, collecting the used breakfast things and taking them over to the sink. And, his back still to her, his voice harsh now, he told her, 'We're to forget your relationship with my father, my knowledge of your lack of morals, are we? Sweep them away under the carpet and pretend they aren't there.' He turned then, his eyes lashing her, almost drawing blood, making her flinch.

'You don't know what you're talking about!' she snarled back at him, her earlier resolves vanishing completely, and he made a slashing movement of his hand, his mouth curling with derision.

'Don't I just? Give me ten minutes alone with you and I'd have you panting to share my bed.'

And that knocked the fight right out of her and she looked down at her hands, her fingers knotted so tightly together that the knuckles showed white. Because it was true, shamingly, horribly true.

And he went on, as if determined to grind her under his heel, 'And don't try to do a whitewash job on yourself because I won't listen. I'd see straight through it, so do yourself a favour and save your breath.'

Imogen lifted her head slowly, her face very pale. As always, with this man, everything had gone wrong. His mood-changes were bewildering, violent. She would never understand him.

Her hope of their being able to forget their differences, or at least to put them into cold storage, and to go on from there to form a viable working relationship which would hopefully, in time, allow her to get her feelings for him sternly under control, had been a non-starter.

Unconsciously, she spread her hands in a small gesture of defeat and, as if that had somehow penetrated his dislike of her, Alex said more gently,

'The proposal you put forward is logical, of course. And it has the benefit of being less wearing on the nervous system.' He gave her a tight, humourless smile. 'I agree.'

'You do?' Her eyes went very wide; she could hardly believe she was hearing him properly. Did he really mean there would be no more downright and hateful insults? No more deliberately flirtatious behaviour and equally deliberate sexual slapdowns the moment he sensed he had successfully brought her to the point of surrender?

'Unreservedly.' He closed the space between them and she stoically ignored the fluttery feeling in her stomach. 'As from now our relationship will be entirely professional and friendly.' He held out a hand. 'Shake on it.'

After a moment's hesitation Imogen took his hand, relieved to find his grip was completely impersonal, but annoyed because long after he had released her her skin still tingled, her nerve-ends retaining the sensual message imparted by skin on warm skin.

But Rome wasn't built in a day, she reminded herself later when she went upstairs to collect her suitcase, then completely outraged herself when, looking back at the beautiful room for the last time, just before she closed the door, she felt her throat tightening with incipient tears because one day soon Alex would be sharing this lovely home with the woman he had promised to marry.

Hating herself for this sign of weakness, she banged the door shut with unnecessary vigour and stuck her chin in the air. She would not give in to the utter futility of wanting, and yes, let's face it, be completely honest about it, of loving a man who was going to marry someone else—a man, moreover, who despised and distrusted her.

Her mouth clamped into a tight line, she marched down the stairs and Alex was waiting for her in the hall, lifting one eyebrow as he took the case from her hand.

'Why the ferocious expression?' he enquired levelly, and she quickly rearranged her face and lied,

'I banged my elbow on the bedroom door.'

He said, very politely, 'You should be more careful. Learn to consider each move you make before you make it. That way you can avoid a lot of grief.'

An ambiguous remark? A warning? Or simply a commonplace pleasantry? She didn't know and wasn't going to try to find out.

Professional and friendly, that was their relationship from now on, she reminded herself, falling in step beside him as he walked across the gravelled apron in front of the house, over the grass between the trees to the courtyard where he'd left his car the evening before.

'I'll want you here first thing in the morning,' he told her as he slid in beside her and fastened his seatbelt. 'And every morning after that until every last pen and paper-clip is in place over there.' He dipped his head in the direction of the outbuildings and Imogen nodded, making a mental note to look up train times. 'You can work from the house, from the study. Tomorrow we'll get down to ordering all the hardware you're going to need.'

'Yes, of course.' She aimed one of her best professional smiles directly through the windscreen while mentally cursing the major hiccup over her usage of the flat. Heaven only knew when she'd find time to look for somewhere to live...

'And now that our relationship's on an entirely new basis, might I make a logical suggestion?' He had pulled the Jaguar on to the main drive from the big house and was easing it towards the road, and he went on smoothly, not waiting for an answer, 'I'd like you to move into Kynaston for the time being, just until the flat's habitable.'

Move in with him? Live in the same house? That, Imogen thought frantically, was taking professional friendship a mite too far! It wouldn't help her resolve to change the way she felt about him one little bit. And she was going to need all the help she could get in that direction!

She tried for a throw-away laugh but it emerged with a shakiness that, even to her own ears, bordered on hysteria.

'I think Tolly should be consulted, don't you? After all, it is his house.'

They were in the town now, pulled up at traffic lights, and his fingers were drumming impatiently against the wheel, his voice grim as he answered, 'You're afraid he might object if he discovered you and I were sharing the same roof?'

That hadn't been what she'd meant, not precisely, and she tried again, unhappily aware that mentioning Tolly at all would have brought all those nasty beliefs of his squirming to the surface of his mind, putting their new agreement in jeopardy much sooner than she'd thought possible. 'As Kynaston is Tolly's property, he might appreciate being consulted about who you invite to take up residence there,' she pointed out, and he shot away as the lights turned green, the growl in his voice echoing that of the engine.

'Let's get one thing straight. I bought Kynaston, not Tolly. So I don't have to consult him, or anyone else, about what happens there. I can invite whomsoever I please to take up residence there—as you put it. But I'm not inviting you, Imogen, I'm telling you.' He shot her a hard look. 'Under the terms of our new agreement there should be no problems. You will have your own self-contained suite, my permission to use the kitchen facilities when and as you need to. You won't have to spend hours each day either travelling or trying to track down some place to live. You are being paid to do a job—and paid very highly, I might add—and I want you on the spot, doing it, not flitting round like a flea in a panic because you've a train to catch or a bed-sit to track down and view. Understand?' he finished, witheringly.

Imogen did, although it was a lot to take in. Alex must have really taken to the house, decided it would make the ideal home to bring his new bride to, and stepped in and bought it over Tolly's head. She might have known that Alexsander Devenko would have too much damned pride to allow his father to pay for his future home.

He must love Catrina very deeply to turn down such a valuable gift simply to have the satisfaction of knowing that he, and he alone, provided for her. And he must know her tastes inside out to have gone ahead, briefed the firm of decorators—even down to the colour of the bed-sheets and bathtowels—without getting her over here for consultations.

The concept didn't make her feel very happy, she acknowledged, feeling a cloud of depression settle on her shoulders, and Alex snapped, reminding her that she should be viewing his suggestion from a merely business viewpoint, 'You can't have any objections, surely?'

'No.' It was as much as she could manage without giving herself away. She could hardly tell him that sharing a roof with him, possibly for the couple of months he had mentioned it might take to render the flat over the stables habitable, would test her resolve to the limits. Or that every time she walked into a room she would be seeing a ghost of the future, a projection of the time when Alex would bring his Catrina to live there as his wife, a time when their children would fill the walls with laughter, race along the corridors and out into the gardens...

CHAPTER EIGHT

'THAT'S beautiful, Mrs Hollins!' Imogen closed the study door behind her, her delighted smile flashing between the elderly daily help and the biggest and brightest Christmas tree she had ever laid eyes on.

Putting the finishing touch to the vivid scarlet ribbon around the base, the stout, grey-haired woman struggled to her feet and put her head on one side consideringly.

'Not bad, though I do say it myself. When Mr Devenko gave me instructions to order a tree—a good one, mind—and decorations to go with it and get it all trimmed out on Christmas Eve, as a surprise for you, I told him I was his woman. Five kids and seven grandchildren, to date—I've had plenty of practice at making a tree look special.'

'And it shows,' Imogen said appreciatively, feeling the sting of tears behind her eyes. Alex had ordered a tree for her, to brighten the festive season, and the gesture touched her more than she could say.

She would be alone here, and he knew that, and he'd taken the trouble to arrange for her day to be brightened. It had been over two weeks since he'd left for the States.

Devenko's business wasn't confined to Europe, of course, and, in a way, she'd been glad to see him go. Since moving into Kynaston, working so closely

with him on the business of the agency, her resolve
to alter the way she felt about him had suffered a
severe set-back.

He'd kept to the letter of their agreement and
she'd found working with him a stimulating experience, and she'd found herself, much against her
firm intentions, falling ever more deeply in love with
him.

So when he'd told her he would be spending
Christmas in the States with his father—and
Catrina, of course, although he hadn't mentioned
her, and why should he, since their relationship was
now strictly business, although friendly?—she had
staunchly informed herself that his taking himself
off was the best possible thing to happen.

'Well, I'd best be going, then. I'll just collect
my coat from the kitchen and get back home.' Mrs
Hollins was untying her pinafore and Imogen
nodded.

'It was good of you to come in at all today—and
happy Christmas to you.' She handed over the en-
velope she'd come out of the study to deliver—a
card and a cheque—and Mrs Hollins said, beaming,

'Oh, you shouldn't have! And best wishes of the
season to you, too, I'm sure. And I'll be in as usual
a couple of days before that party you're having
on New Year's Eve, only should you need me before
just get in touch. You've got my phone number.'

Watching her waddle away, Imogen shook her
head, smiling slightly. There would be little point
in telling her to take a full week off, that staff were
being hired specially for the New Year house-
warming party.

As far as Mrs Hollins was concerned, anything that went on in Kynaston was her business, and any outside staff were going to know it! Imogen didn't know how or where Alex had managed to find such a treasure, but she had arrived the day after Imogen had moved in, her pinafore and indoor shoes in a big plastic bag, her intention to take over the domestic running of the house, and the rather rough-and-ready mothering of Imogen herself, becoming patently clear within the hour!

Alone, Imogen walked all round the tree, fingering the glittering gold and silver baubles, the scarlet tinsel, swallowing the lump in her throat. There had been a time when she had hated Christmas, the unhappiness of her home life showing up more starkly at that special time of the year.

But she was over that now. She didn't hate it; she merely felt lonely.

Turning her back on the tree which took pride of place in the hall, she ran up the stairs and fetched an old anorak and her boots from her room. It was early afternoon and, her work finished until the agency began functioning fully at the start of the new year, she had to find some way to occupy herself.

She would go for a walk, a long one, stay out until the last of the light faded from the sky, then make a fire in the huge fireplace in the hall and sit and admire her Christmas tree. She would not allow herself to be miserable!

It was cold and still outside, the sky a heavy pewter-grey, and she instinctively huddled deeper inside her anorak and wondered whether to turn right round and light the fire she'd promised herself this very minute. But she was made of sterner stuff than that, she reminded herself with a tight smile. Exercise she needed, and exercise was what she was going to get!

There was a door in one of the walls that bounded the courtyard around the one-time stable block and outbuildings, and beyond it, she knew, was a secluded lane where she could walk for miles, and she made for it, cutting across the grass and through the trees.

The studios were complete now, right down to the draughting-tables, typewriters, fax machine, and she was itching to really get down to work. She already had several campaign ideas and had discussed them with Alex, who had been openly impressed. She could hardly wait until after the New Year house-warming party—to which all the new agency staff were invited—to get round the table with her team, toss her ideas around, and start to get them into production.

Surely, when she was properly and completely engrossed in her new and highly responsible job, she would be too busy and involved to have time to moon over her impossible love for Alex, and her feelings for him would fade until they became nothing more than the memory of a distant time when, foolishly, she had allowed her emotions to swamp her common sense.

The sound of hammering grew louder as she approached the courtyard and she paused in her stride, her head tilted. A distant male voice called out, to be answered by a derisory hoot of laughter, and someone else was whistling tunelessly.

Work had progressed on the flat she was to use at a rate that had privately astounded her, but she hadn't expected anyone to be working on it today—not with Christmas only a few hours away.

Only a few weeks ago Alex had told her that the flat wouldn't be habitable for a couple of months at least, but lately the gang of craftsmen—plasterers, plumbers, tilers, electricians—had put in a lot of overtime. She could only surmise that Alex and Catrina had at last named the day, that it would be soon. They would not want her lodging at Kynaston.

And that suited her fine, she told herself staunchly. She would be far happier in a place of her own. She certainly didn't want to make an unwanted third when Alex proudly brought his new bride home.

Shrugging off an unwelcome feeling of depression, she emerged from the grove of trees and, sure enough, lights shone through the open windows of her future home and someone emptied a bucket of old plaster out of one of them into the waiting skip below.

Deciding to make a short detour and view work in progress—after all, the flat was to be her home—she mounted the stone steps, pushed open the door and walked into the foreman who was sitting on a bucket, pouring tea from a Thermos.

'I'm sorry, Alf!' she exclaimed, seeing half the tea soak into his dust-covered overalls, and his glower was exchanged for a wide grin.

'Oh, it's you, miss. Not to worry; plenty more where that came from. Like a cup?'

'No, thanks.' She shook her head. 'I just dropped in to see how you were getting on. Didn't expect anyone to be working today.'

'He would have had us working all day tomorrow, too. Only, the chaps won't stand for that. Mind you, he's handing over a whopping great bonus if we finish before New Year.' Alf stood up, draining what was left of his tea, screwing the top back on the Thermos. 'He' was obviously Alex, and he must want her out of Kynaston on the double!

Refusing to dwell on the implications of that, she asked with assumed brightness, 'Do you think you'll make it?'

'Got no choice.' The foreman wiped his mouth with the back of his hand and yelled an instruction to a youth who was wandering around with a can of paint, then pulled a wry face at Imogen. 'Place to be completed by the thirtieth, no messing. There's a couple of blokes—those foreigners who's coming over here to work—so the place has to be ready for them to move in. Mind you, like I said, he's not stingy with his orders but he's not stingy with his pay, either. Want to take a look round, then?'

Again Imogen shook her head and, over the sudden panicky constriction in her throat, she managed, 'Vinet and Stein will be living here?' and Alf grunted,

'That's right. Those were the names of the blokes he mentioned. Sure you don't want to take a look?'

'No—I'm supposed to be taking a walk,' she said, edging back towards the door, her mind woolly.

Alf disappeared through one of the open doors, grunting, 'Rather you than me; it's cold enough to bring tears to your eyes out there!' and she let herself out, closing the door gently behind her, walking down the stone steps, her legs feeling distinctly shaky.

What in the name of heaven was going on? She'd been promised the use of the flat, and no one had told her any differently. Letting herself through the door in the wall, she pushed her hands into the pockets of her anorak, bent her head against the suddenly rising wind, and walked briskly down the lane.

She thought better on her feet but her thoughts weren't pleasant companions. The spacious flat would be ideal for two bachelors; she could see that. But where would she go, and why hadn't Alex told her of his altered plans?

He and Catrina certainly wouldn't want her at Kynaston after they were married; the arrangement had only been temporary, in any case, just until the flat was ready for her to move into. And when she'd last asked him if he'd managed to find accommodation locally for Pierre and Stefan he'd merely told her not to·fret, that he had everything in hand.

And the only conclusion she could draw was that, despite their new accord, the agreement they had struck and kept to, Alex was up to something, beavering away to get her thrown out of the firm.

He still resented her for what he believed to be her affair with his father, her unfair acquisition of the job he had earmarked for Pierre Vinet. He would stop short of nothing to get her removed, she thought with a shudder.

He had once warned her against underestimating him, informed her that those who had done so in the past had lived to regret it. And on another occasion he had advised her to consider each move before she made it. She had thought at the time that it had been a strangely ambiguous remark.

Her move to Kynaston had been a bad mistake and she certainly hadn't considered the implications of giving up her independence. If he succeeded in removing her from the company she would not only be without a job but without a home. And how she could love such a devious devil she couldn't imagine!

But no one fell in love to order, she thought miserably, shivering as a particularly vicious gust of wind went straight through her. Love was illogical, without rhyme or reason, and she couldn't explain, not even to herself, why just one man in the whole world could appeal to her so deeply, making her lose all that emotional control she'd built up so carefully over the years.

Miserably, she glanced up at the sky. It was darkening quite dramatically and she had walked much further than she'd meant to. And, as she turned to retrace her steps, the first snowflakes fell, driven on the back of the biting wind.

It would be a traditional white Christmas, she thought with a pang. And she would have no one to share it with.

But longing for Alex, wishing that things were different, was a futile waste of energy, and, after telling herself that it was too soon to jump to conclusions about his allocating the flat she had been promised to Stefan and Pierre, at least before she'd had the opportunity to talk to Alex himself about it, she relentlessly pushed him to the far recesses of her mind and began the long walk back to Kynaston.

Imogen was bitterly cold by the time she let herself in through the back door, snow plastering the front of her anorak, her skirt wet through and sticking to her legs, one of her knees deeply grazed where she'd blundered into a low stone wall in the darkness.

Her fingers numb with cold, she wearily removed the sodden anorak and draped it over a chair in front of the electric Aga. The temptation to give way under the weight of depression that had been growing heavier ever since she'd spoken to Alf earlier this afternoon was almost irresistible.

But she managed to shake it off, telling herself that her present miserable state was all her own fault. She shouldn't have walked so far and she should have kept a closer eye on the weather conditions, on the onset of darkness; she shouldn't have wallowed in bitter introspection over Alex's possible motives for going back on his promise to let her have the flat.

She would have a hot bath, attend to her grazed knee, build that fire she'd promised herself and have a lazy, relaxed evening. And she would refuse to let Alexsander Devenko into her mind!

But the sound of the wall-mounted phone sent her determination not to even think of him flying out of her head, and her heart was pattering with hope as she limped over to answer it. But Tolly's voice came loud and clear, all the way from New York, and her heart dropped down into her soggy boots. Just for one moment she had been so sure that Alex would phone, if only to wish her the compliments of the season.

'I'm absolutely fine, and no, I don't mind in the least spending Christmas on my own,' she replied to his questions, a little less than truthfully.

'Pleased to hear it,' Tolly chuckled, then, 'We're having a huge family get-together over here,' and Imogen closed her eyes against a sudden, weak sting of tears. He hadn't meant to be unkind, rub salt in the wound of her loneliness, surely he hadn't. Tolly wasn't like that.

And after she'd answered his detailed questions concerning the new agency he told her,

'I'm really looking forward to being back in London, getting to grips with the designers and architects for the new store. Alex tells me I should leave it all to him, tries to tell me I work too hard, but that's nonsense. I'm not in my dotage yet!'

He sounded very cheerful and Imogen wondered what he'd say if she told him what really lay behind Alex's desire to keep him away from London—that he was doing his damnedest to keep his father out of the clutches of a greedy little gold-digger!

For a moment she debated whether to tell him or not; on the one hand it would mean that Tolly could finally tell the truth that Alex was patently unable to believe when it came from her, and on the other hand there was a very real fear that it would cause a row between father and son, spoil the holiday for them.

And then the decision was taken right out of her hands when Tolly, saying goodbye, took the breath right out of her lungs as he added, 'See you at the house-warming next week, my dear—and, before I forget, we'll be bringing Catrina over, so mind you get one of the prettiest rooms ready for her!'

There wouldn't be much point, was Imogen's first numbing thought. However pretty the room prepared for her, Catrina wouldn't be sleeping in it—Alex would see to that!

Pushing herself up the stairs on legs that felt like lumps of lead, Imogen wondered how she would be able to stand it. How could she bear to stay under the same roof as Alex and his bride-to-be?

But the news shouldn't have come as such a shock, she told herself tartly as she ran her bath. She should have foreseen that Catrina would naturally be present at the house-warming of her future home, and done something about it. She could have invented friends in the far north of Scotland, with whom she had promised to spend Christmas and the New Year, and removed herself altogether.

But she hadn't, and must suffer the consequences of her own short-sightedness, and she couldn't even phone her mother in Athens and beg her to invite her to spend the holiday there because she, Imogen, had already promised to organise the house party at Kynaston and she never reneged on her promises.

So she would just have to grit her teeth and pretend to enjoy herself, wouldn't she? she informed her reflected image in the mirrored wall of the bathroom. Belting the towelling robe, she stuffed her feet into mules and pushed her fingers through her rough-dried hair.

There was little point in getting dressed again for a quiet evening on her own; she would make herself a scratch meal, put a light to the fire in the hall and curl up in the armchair with the Christmas tree and the new thick paperback she'd bought in Windsor yesterday for company.

But Imogen couldn't bring herself to eat the beef sandwiches she'd cut herself and, try as she might, she couldn't get beyond the first page of her favourite author's latest bestseller. The cheerful crackling of the fire only emphasised the silence and the glittering tree only reminded her of Alex, putting him firmly back in her head, which was precisely where she didn't want him to be.

The best place for her was bed, she decided grimly, then went very still, her skin prickling as she heard someone fumbling around outside the front door, the sound of a key scraping into the lock.

Several people knew that Kynaston would be empty over the holiday, except for herself, and that she would be no match for a determined burglar;

and there were many fine antiques here, quite apart from Alex's collection of valuable paintings—a collection he'd made over the years and had had brought over from a Paris bank vault shortly after he'd moved in here.

Cursing herself because she hadn't yet activated the alarm system, something she regularly did before she went to bed, Imogen shot to her feet and looked wildly around for something to defend herself with.

Then the door swung open and Alex was there, snow plastering his dark head, his heavy sheepskin, and weak tears of relief sprang to her eyes and she said, her voice a whispery wobble, 'It's you!'

'Who were you expecting? Santa?' His grin melted her bones; simply seeing him again sent wave after wave of delirious happiness crashing through her and she was still in shock after thinking she was about to be attacked, the house stripped of its valuables.

Unable to dissemble, her whole heart was in her violet eyes as she told him, 'When you opened the door I expected a couple of thugs to walk in. Am I glad to see you!'

'So I can take it I'm slightly more welcome than a couple of felons.' He was still smiling, walking towards her now, leaving clumps of melting snow on the rugs that were scattered over the floor; but his eyes sobered as he stood in front of her, noting her pallor, the slight tremors that shook the slender body beneath the towelling robe.

'I frightened you,' he said with husky contrition, his arms gathering her against his body. 'I'm a fool. I did think of phoning you from the airport, to warn you, but decided to surprise you instead. The weather was atrocious and even a delay of ten minutes could have made the difference between getting here and getting stranded. I meant to surprise you,' he murmured against her hair, 'not frighten you half to death.'

As an apology it was fulsome, and he could give her the fright of her life as often as he liked if it meant he would hold her gently like this, so close to him.

She was still trembling—not for the reason he imagined, but because being in his arms like this made her emotions run riot. And she heard him mutter self-denigratingly as he released her and shrugged out of his wet coat.

'Stay here by the fire,' he instructed tersely. 'I'll fetch you some brandy; you look as if you need it.'

'No.' Imogen shook her head, her pale, silky hair flying around her face. She didn't need alcohol, his unexpected presence here was intoxicating enough. And he gave her a hard look.

'Don't worry, I'm not about to get you drunk again, even though the consequences of doing so are tempting.'

Instinctively, her hands went up to cover her face, to hide the pain and humiliation. Why did he have to bring that up again? Why, when only moments ago he'd been so gentle, so caring?

'Hell!' The expletive seemed torn from him and he took hold of her wrists to pull her hands from her face. 'What am I doing to you? Imogen——' his golden eyes met hers with fierce intensity '—I've flown thousands of miles to be with you, and my anger at myself for scaring you senseless is making me snipe at you. Forgive me?'

His fingers were caressing the racing pulse-points on her inner wrists, and his eyes, the deep warmth of his voice, were hypnotising her, and she knew she must have misheard him.

Alex wouldn't, couldn't have flown in so late on Christmas Eve to be with her—not when he'd planned to spend the holiday with Tolly and Catrina. It simply didn't make sense. There must have been an urgent business problem to do with Devenko's London to have brought him here. So, to set the record straight, to stop the crazy pounding of her heart, she asked thickly, 'Why are you here?'

'I told you,' he said with husky emphasis, 'to be with you.' He looked deeply into her eyes and brought her hands up to his mouth, turning them over and placing soft kisses in each palm, and the heated excitement that washed through her made her melt inside, and he pulled her closer by her wrists and their bodies were touching and she could feel the heavy beat of his heart beneath her breasts.

He made a soft, almost inaudible sound deep in his throat and she knew he was going to kiss her, and could do nothing to stop it. Didn't want to stop it. Her mouth parted in a soft invitation that she had no control over whatsoever and his lips took hers with a fierce male pressure that had her arms twining around his neck, her fingers sliding through his hair.

Her entire being trembled beneath the sensual onslaught as her body was pressed ever more closely to his, making her recognise the extent of his arousal, and she knew she was where she had always wanted to be, close to him, loving him, and as his hands impatiently pushed her robe aside and found the taut globes of her naked breasts she felt him tremble, heard him whisper raggedly,

'I've wanted this for so long!'

A small cry of pleasure was torn from her as she felt the moist heat of his mouth against her breast, and she arched her back in mindless invitation, everything forgotten in her need for the man she loved. And as her legs refused to support her she felt him lower her to the soft, thick hearth-rug and went with him willingly, the robe that had somehow been completely discarded lying beneath her.

'You are so beautiful.' Alex was beside her, propped up on one elbow, one fingertip tracing the exquisite lines of her body in the warm play of the flickering firelight. 'I've dreamed of seeing you like this. Night after night I've dreamed of it. I thought I was going out of my mind.'

Her slumbrous eyes fixed lovingly on the passionate line of his mouth, she asked huskily, 'How long have you wanted me?'

It was the age-old question from a woman in love, and he said thickly, 'From the first moment I saw you.' His hand was smoothing the delicate line of her flanks and all she could concentrate on was the utterly new and devastating sensation he was arousing—that, and the dark flush of naked desire that suffused his well-loved face, so that when he added, 'I rushed over from Paris to put an end to your affair with Tolly and promptly disgusted myself by being jealous as hell. Jealous of my own

father!' it took her some moments to grasp the
import of what he'd said. And she whispered
worriedly, just as he dropped a lingering kiss on
the soft inner curve of her hip,

'Tolly and I were never lovers. Never came near
it. You have to believe me.'

'Sure. Sure, sweetheart——' His mouth was
trailing a line of fire across the plane of her
stomach, filling her with a wild and wanton
yearning. 'I gave you a bad time, but it's all forgotten now.'

He drew away from her, but only to begin to
remove his own clothing and his voice was a deep
promise of ecstasy to come as he gathered her in
his arms and stopped anything else she might have
said, his mouth over hers as he murmured, 'Don't
talk, my love, not now. You and I have far better
things to do.'

CHAPTER NINE

IMOGEN came awake slowly, drifting back to consciousness through layer on layer of exquisite dreams.

No, not dreams, she realised, not dreams at all, but wonderful reality. Alex loving her, Alex carrying her up here to lay her tenderly on the elegant half-tester bed that took pride of place in his bedroom, making love to her again and again, making her senses run riot, making her want to cry for the beauty of loving and giving and being loved in return.

Stirring languidly in the warm depths of the bed, she reached out an arm and curled it around his sleeping body. Several times last night he had said he loved her, his voice ragged with emotion as he shuddered violently beneath her untutored caresses. It was like magic, too amazing to be believed.

Dropping a soft kiss on his tousled dark head, she slid carefully out of bed, letting him sleep, and went quickly along the silent corridor to her own room.

Last night had been almost too perfect; she couldn't quite get to grips with the implications of what had happened. But a few minutes under the stinging, hot jets of the shower cleared her mind and she was frowning slightly as she wrapped herself in a large fern-green towel.

Everything had happened so quickly, his assault on her senses too devastating to be withstood. He had always been able to make her want him and last night she had been particularly vulnerable. They had wanted each other so desperately that there hadn't been time to talk, there hadn't seemed to be a need to discuss anything at all—whispered words of love had said it all.

But he had seemed to accept that there had never been anything except friendship between herself and his father—at least she thought he did, although her memory wasn't too clear on what had actually been said. He had almost seemed to dismiss her statement about her relationship with Tolly, as if it was no longer of any importance.

It wasn't that that was bothering her so much, though, and she knotted her brows as ferociously as she knotted the towel above her breasts while she walked back through to her bedroom, her mouth dropping open as she saw Alex lounging back on her bed, his arms crossed behind his head, wearing nothing at all.

He was utterly beautiful, a superb male animal in prime condition, and her mouth went dry, and the now familiar melting sensation weakened her limbs as he smiled at her lazily, one dark brow arching as he warned softly, 'Don't do that again. I thought you'd run out on me. I want to find you right there beside me when I wake, each and every morning. Come here.'

She did no such thing, ignoring the sexual invitation with difficulty, standing her ground, her violet eyes troubled, and he swung himself to a sitting position, his long, hair-roughened legs over the edge of the bed.

'Come——' he patted the space at his side, his face gentle with concern '—tell me what's wrong.'

She went to him then, pattering quickly into the warm, safe haven of his arms, snuggling tight against his body, and he stroked the long, silky fall of her hair, his dark voice soft.

'Tell me, sweetheart.'

'It's Catrina,' she muttered, her head on his shoulder, her lips brushing against the corded strength of his neck, and although there was a painful lump in her throat she promised herself she wouldn't cry, at least not in front of him, when he said—as she fully expected he would—that Catrina had nothing to do with any of this, that because their engagement had been so long he felt fully entitled to take a mistress from time to time.

But he said nothing, just continued to stroke her hair as if soothing a troubled child, and she wondered if perhaps, after all, he had a conscience, already regretted what had happened between them, regretted having cheated on the woman he really loved, the woman he was going to marry.

So, taking her flagging courage in both hands, she muttered miserably, 'You're engaged to marry her,' and hated herself utterly because she had known that all along, hadn't she? Known it and had still given in to the way she felt about him, the desperate need to have him possess her.

'Don't cry,' he said, a husky break in his voice as his fingers unerringly found the trail of wetness down her cheeks. And she didn't know how he had guessed at the silently falling tears that, despite all her good intentions, she hadn't been able to prevent. 'One of the reasons I went back to New York was to break the engagement.'

Her heart leapt upwards. So he was free. She hadn't been guilty of making love with a man who was already committed, and he cupped her face with his hands, his eyes loving her as he told her gently, 'The engagement should never have happened in the first place. Our parents wanted it more than we did. At the time, I wanted to please Tolly more than anything else; he'd been having a particularly harrowing——'

He broke off, his mouth wry. 'Never mind the reasons behind it. At that time I'd never happened across a woman I wanted to share the rest of my life with, and a marriage between Catrina and myself seemed sensible, for various reasons. She's a beautiful girl, highly intelligent, very poised, and would make any man a marvellous wife. But neither of us was in love with the other, which was why the engagement went on so long. And, at the time it was mooted, neither of us really thought we'd find anyone we would end up loving more than life itself.'

His beautiful voice was mesmeric, and Imogen felt her breath catch in her throat as he lowered his mouth to cover hers, and later, as he gently untangled his legs from hers, he smiled down into her hazy eyes and demanded softly, 'Promise you won't leave me. Ever. I want you here with me, always.'

'A live-in lover?' she asked with a quirk of her lips, trying to make light of something she would have to think long and hard about. She loved him to the point of desperation but didn't think she could face it if he ever tired of her and walked out of her life.

The longer she stayed with him the deeper her dependence would grow, the stronger the danger of what would happen to her if she lost him.

But she needed time to think about it, so she tossed him a teasing smile and stretched languorously. 'I've always fancied being a kept woman.'

'No chance!' He brushed her jaw with his fist. 'You'll be earning yourself a fat salary with the agency, but staying right here. Why do you think I manoeuvred you into a corner about where you should live?'

'And allocated my flat to Pierre and Stefan!' she stated with mock anger, pummelling his broad, naked chest with small, ineffectual fists. 'Did you never even consider that I might actually like my independence?'

It all began to slot into place. She had been hurt, hadn't been able to understand why the flat she had been promised had been given to the others. He must have been very determined to make her his lover. What Alexsander Devenko wanted, Alexsander Devenko got!

The thought of being the subject of such single-minded determination made her shudder. And he watched the tremor pass through her body, saw the way her eyes darkened in a way that was almost panic-stricken, and said lazily, 'So you know about that. Don't worry, if you're afraid I'm trying to tie you down to marriage, forget it. I know how you feel about it, and I respect those feelings. So don't throw a moody on me——' He scooped her up in his arms and lifted her off the bed. 'It's Christmas day and I've a couple of things to show you.'

Imogen had forgotten it was Christmas and she swallowed the constriction in her throat and did her best to join in his obvious pleasure as he led her over to the window.

She couldn't tell him that since falling in love with him she had reversed her opinions on the state of matrimony. She would marry him tomorrow, spend the rest of her life loving him, happily allow the emotions that he had called back to life to colour and enrich all their days together.

But he had said he didn't want to marry her, and his long, abortive engagement to Catrina pointed to an in-built aversion on his part to the idea of such a long-term and serious commitment. Her earlier confession that her parents' marriage had put her off the idea for life had probably been the first step in his realisation that they had a great deal in common!

But as he drew back the heavy yellow linen curtains she bit back a deep sense of disappointment and gazed with wide eyes at the scene before her.

Snow lay thickly everywhere, pristine and untouched, the early sun glittering on the frozen surface with a million diamond points of pink and amber light, and Alex said, 'A perfect, fairy-tale Christmas morning. Let's pretend it was created especially for us.' And she blinked back foolish tears because it would be nice to believe just that, to think that the heavens had smiled on them and had made this, their first Christmas together, so very special.

That it might be their last together was something she refused to think about just now and when he said,

'Get dressed. And if you get down first and make breakfast you can see what else I've got to show you, just as a reward!' she abandoned herself to his light-hearted mood.

Although she didn't linger over dressing, choosing to wear soft cord cream-coloured trousers topped by a loose-fitting rich purple mohair sweater, leaving her long pale hair loose and contenting herself with just a shadow of eye make-up and a shimmer of soft pink lipstick, he was down before her, turning the bacon under the grill.

And his eyes were dark with desire as he turned to watch her walk across the room and a catch of emotion made his voice husky as he chided, 'Slouch! But I'll forgive you—I'll allow you to look in the box, even if you have condemned me to a hot stove.'

The gift-wrapped box wasn't big but she couldn't have missed it. It took pride of place in the centre of the kitchen table, the huge crimson and silver bow on top of it larger than the box itself.

'Well, go on—open it,' he commanded as she was still grinning at the over-the-top decoration, so she did, her breath catching in her throat when she saw the perfect oval amethyst suspended by a fine gold chain.

'Like it?' he asked offhandedly, cracking eggs into the frying-pan, and Imogen tenderly lifted the pendant from its white velvet bed and turned to him, her eyes full of love.

'It's beautiful,' she whispered huskily. 'But I haven't got anything for you.' She felt bad about that but he smiled crookedly, dropped the spoon he'd been using to baste the eggs and said,

'Come here, woman,' and she went to him, still holding the pendant, and he took it from her, turning her, fastening the fine chain around her neck. 'I bought it because it's the exact colour of your fantastic eyes. It's not as beautiful, of course, but then, nothing ever could be.'

He had said something very similar when he'd handed her the rose he'd bought from the flower-seller in Paris, and she had fallen in love with him that evening, and a *frisson* of intense emotion ran through her and she turned in his arms, and he held her, one hand in her hair, his fingers threading through its silky length, his voice rough as he told her, 'As a gift, that stone's a paltry thing beside the gift you've already given me. You've given me yourself, and as far as I'm concerned that's the most priceless thing in the world.'

It was almost too much to take and she gratefully seized on the excuse of the smell of burning to twist out of his arms, lighten the emotions that were long on intensity and short on long-term commitment, permanence, rescuing the grill-pan and nudging the sizzling frying-pan away from the heat.

'I'm too hungry to risk ruining breakfast,' she fibbed, smiling up at him, and he flicked the end of her nose with his finger, drawling laconically,

'Nothing will be ruined for us today. I won't let it be.'

And he was right; the day had been utterly perfect, Imogen reflected dreamily as she sipped her champagne, feeling the warmth of the crackling wood fire on her face.

After breakfast they had wrapped up in warm anoraks, pulled on boots and set out for a walk in the glittering fairyland world outside, ending up in the paddock making a monster of a snowman, a slight difference of opinion over who the creation most resembled ending up in a snow fight which had them both plastered from head to foot with the cold, clinging crystals, subsiding into each other's arms, out of breath and weak with laughter.

Running back to the house through the snow, hand in hand like irresponsible children, was something Imogen would never forget. She felt far younger and far more carefree than she had ever done as a child.

If Alex tired of her tomorrow she would still, in a small part of her mind that was not perpetually grieving, thank him for teaching her to admit that the emotions played just as important a part in life as common sense and logic.

But that small, looming cloud was quickly dispersed when Alex decided that, after stripping off their sodden clothes, a hot bath was called for. Shared, of course.

'Got a mean streak, have you?' she questioned seriously, very wide-eyed. 'Does the thought of wasting hot water on two baths give you goosebumps?' She hadn't been able to hide the impish smile that tugged at her mouth and it shone forth in full radiance when he answered with a growl,

'To hell with wasting water, woman! What gives me goose-bumps is the thought of wasting one precious moment away from you!'

And later they had listened to a carol service on the radio as they'd pottered round the kitchen, sipping red wine and preparing dinner. The small chicken Imogen had bought to cook for herself was eked out by the smoked salmon Alex brought from the deep freeze and the mince pies Mrs Hollins had made for her.

Alex had lit the fire in the hall again and together they'd carried a small circular pedestal table from the sitting-room, setting it between the fire and the glittering tree; and he'd chilled a bottle of champagne, and his eyes had told her how lovely he found her so that she knew her efforts to look beautiful for him had not been in vain, the smoky-grey chiffon dress she'd only worn once before, for the launch party of the 'Jewels' perfumery range, making her look ethereal and mysterious.

The last log flared up, crackled briefly, then fell with a whisper on to its soft bed of ash, and Alex stood up, heart-stoppingly attractive in his black dinner-jacket, holding his hand out to her across the table.

'Come to bed, my love, come to me.'

And Imogen rose to her feet, her full skirts drifting softly around her slender legs like the slowly fluttering wings of a moth, and laid her hand in his, willing to go with him always, wherever he went, whatever he asked of her.

*   *   *

The days went by, in a way timeless, in another way slipping past far too quickly, like grains of sand through careless fingers.

Imogen had made all the arrangements for the house-warming party, which was also to be a celebration of the opening of the new agency and the beginning of the long haul to the opening of Devenko's London.

The guest-list was small, but everything had to be perfect and outside staff and caterers had been hired for the party itself.

Pierre Vinet and Stefan Stein would be staying on until the flat over the stables had been furnished, a matter of only a few days, and although Cathy Ames would stay for the night of the party she would be moving in with her aunt in Ascot the following day.

The other overnight guests were Tom Fisher, the chief architect for the new store, who was, apparently, a personal friend of Tolly's, plus his wife Monica.

All well and good, Imogen thought, frowning over the list of rooms allocated, but she hadn't been told to expect Catrina. And Alex, leaning over her shoulder and dropping a kiss on the lobe of her ear, asked, 'Problems, precious?'

He had just come in from inspecting the finished work over at the flat and he smelled good, of crisp, fresh air and virile male, and she smiled up at him. 'Tolly phoned on Christmas Eve and said Catrina would be coming with him for the house-warming.'

She chewed on a corner of her lip; she still didn't know how she felt about meeting Catrina tomorrow. Had the ending of the long-standing engagement been as amicable as Alex had intimated?

'And her mother, 'Stasia,' Alex said, seemingly totally unconcerned. 'Where's your problem?'

'Rooms,' she ground out succinctly, running her fingers through the hair she usually left loose these days because Alex preferred it that way, wondering how many more people she didn't know about would be arriving.

'Should be enough.' He was tugging off his sheepskin coat and he dropped it on one end of the long kitchen table and walked over to where Imogen was sitting, frowning over her list. 'Let's see.' Scooping her up from the chair, he sat down, settling her on his knees, scanning the list without much apparent interest. 'You've given Vinet and Stein a room each—they can share a twin-bedded; Cathy Ames in the small single, Tolly and the Fishers stay put, and Catrina and her mother can share the room you used to have. Simple.'

His strong arms tightened around her and he nuzzled his face against her neck, tasting her skin. She said tartly, 'And if they have my room, where am I supposed to sleep?'

'With me, of course.' His sharp teeth nipped her earlobe. 'Where else?'

Imogen went very still, her breath sticking in her lungs, and felt her face go red. And, as if he felt her withdrawal, he slid one hand beneath her loose sweater, cupping her breast. It filled his palm just perfectly, and, before she forgot everything else in the wild slaking of a desire only he could arouse, and so effortlessly, too, she pushed his hand away and slid off his lap.

'We could book Cathy into an hotel in Windsor for the night; I'm sure she wouldn't mind,' she suggested coolly, almost hating him for the mocking glints that appeared in his eyes. 'I don't think our sharing a room would be entirely tactful, do you? Not under the circumstances.'

'What circumstances?' No sign of golden, mocking lights now; his eyes had narrowed, hardened, his mouth a straight line.

'You've only recently broken your engagement to Catrina, and what would Tolly think? He——' She broke off, shaking her head.

They both knew that the elderly man had set his heart on that marriage; they both knew how disappointed he must be to see his rosy dreams shattered. But to spell it out would only make Alex feel guilty. But he didn't look guilty; he looked icily angry as he bit out, standing up and towering over her, 'And what the hell has Tolly got to do with the way you and I feel about each other?'

And Imogen's eyes widened with shock because they were back to fighting again, and she could see the bitter accusation in his eyes—surely he couldn't still think she'd been sleeping with his father for what she could get out of him? Oh, surely not!

'Nothing,' she denied miserably, hating to think he should believe the worst of her. 'I love you.'

'Then damn well prove it!' He looked as if he wanted to hit her, a muscle working furiously at the side of his jaw, and to her intense annoyance she felt tears well in her eyes.

She would never have believed she could be so weak, and hated herself for it. He was the only person in the world who could make her so over-emotional, and he snapped at her, his eyes narrowed slits, 'Are you ashamed of our relationship?'

Ashamed? How could she ever be ashamed of loving him, of expressing that love in a way that felt so right, so natural? She shook her head slowly, her eyes on his, and heard him make a small, rough sound in the back of his throat as he covered the space to where she stood, his arms enfolding her, dragging her into the length of his body as he told her raggedly, 'Never try to hide what we feel. Never! I want the whole world to know you're my woman. I'm proud of it and if you love me you'll be proud of it too.'

After that there was no question of her doing anything other than share his bed. Not that she wanted to do anything else, but she had been concerned about how Tolly, so recently disappointed by the broken engagement, would view the situation.

And after all, she rationalised as she and Alex greeted the guests and showed them to their rooms, how many people lurked around passages at night, watching to see who shared with whom?

She would hate for Tolly to resent her, believe she was directly responsible for the broken engagement. She knew now, from things Alex had told her, that he and Catrina would never have married. The length of the engagement had been due to inertia, he'd said, the failure of either one of them to fall in love with someone else, plus a misguided sense of family duty.

In fact, he had told her that right at the beginning of the engagement they had made a pact to release each other if either felt, for whatever reason, he or she wanted to end it—no questions and no hard feelings on either side.

'What a perfectly lovely room!' Monica Fisher exclaimed as Imogen opened the door to the spacious bedroom, decorated in shades of peacock-blue and aquamarine, with two sets of windows overlooking the gardens at the back of the house, snow still lingering against north-facing walls. And her husband, Tom, quite a few years older than his elegant wife, Imogen judged, put an overnight case on the chest at the foot of the bed and commented easily,

'Alex always did have excellent taste. He's been responsible for the décor of the stores for the past ten years or more—on top of being the financial brain behind the business.'

'And good taste in women,' Monica tacked on, her head on one side as she smiled at Imogen in open approval, and before the other woman could say any more Imogen said quickly,

'I'll leave you to it. Tea will be ready in the hall in about half an hour,' and left them with a poised smile that was totally at odds with the churning of her feelings.

How on earth did they know that she and Alex were an item? The couple had only been in the house for ten minutes, arriving with Tolly, 'Stasia and Catrina, having picked them up from the airport earlier. Did what they felt for each other show so very clearly?

Yet Pierre and Stefan, arriving together before lunch that morning, had given no indication that they sensed anything, Imogen recalled. Pierre, incorrigible as ever, had gone out of his way to flirt with her, drawing quite a few frowns from Alex! Surely he wouldn't have stuck his neck out so far if he'd picked up vibes telling him that his boss and his new agency manager were in love with each other?

Trying to dismiss the conundrum from her mind, she hurried downstairs. Pierre and Stefan had spent the afternoon at the studio premises and looking at the flat that was to be their new home, and they would be back in no time at all for the lavish English tea Mrs Hollins was preparing, no doubt getting in the way of the hired staff who were busy with the food for this evening's party, she thought on a sigh.

And Cathy's train didn't arrive at Windsor until just after five, and, although Alex had said he would collect her, Imogen thought she should offer, if only to give him more time with his father who, Imogen considered, had looked dreadfully tired on arrival.

She was totally lost in her thoughts as she hurried across the hall, first checking that the fire was not in need of fresh logs, and almost fell over herself in surprise when a hand on her arm and a cool voice stayed her.

Catrina had slid up behind her, silently, rather like a snake, Imogen thought, settling back into her shoes and finding a smile.

'Sorry to make you jump,' the other girl apologised, her voice sinuous and soft, reinforcing the
snake-like image given by the tight black garment
that clung to her reed-thin body.

Imogen shook her head to clear it of her idiotic
thoughts. When she'd arrived, Catrina had greeted
her with every appearance of friendliness, apparently not one whit put out at meeting the woman
who had been sharing her one-time fiancé's home
for the past few weeks.

And there had been no antagonism between her
and Alex; indeed, they had treated each other like
old and valued friends, and she'd chattered away
most amicably to her erstwhile husband-to-be as
Alex had taken it on himself to show her and her
mother, and Tolly, to the rooms they were to use.

'I didn't see you,' Imogen apologised in turn. 'I
was miles away, wondering how Mrs Hollins was
getting on with the English tea she's been recklessly
promising all day—toast and Gentlemen's Relish,
hot English muffins, and honey, of course.'

She was babbling, and that wasn't like her, but
something about the cool glint of Catrina's vivid
green eyes unsettled her. She couldn't put her finger
on it precisely, but...

'If you can spare just five minutes from your
domestic trials, I would rather like a word with
you,' Catrina said silkily, her voice barely above a
whisper. 'Perhaps the study?' She began to move
down the hall, her painted finger-nails still digging
into Imogen's arm and, annoyed by the arbitrary
abduction, Imogen dug her heels in.

'Perhaps later? I do have a lot to do, I'm afraid.' She didn't want to be rude, not exactly, but something about the other girl's smile was sending shivers down her spine and, besides, she couldn't imagine what Catrina, who had only been introduced to her half an hour or so ago, could possibly have to say that couldn't wait.

'Later might be too late,' Catrina smiled enigmatically. 'I've taken a liking to you, you know. I do that all the time—take immediate likes or dislikes.' Her eyebrows rose as if her own idiosyncrasies took her by surprise, then she tilted her head on one side and produced a radiant smile. 'And I've decided that I can't, just can't, stand by and see you hurt. Abused. And what I can tell you, warn you against, will stop that happening. Interested?'

CHAPTER TEN

IMOGEN decided it would be easier to humour her, less time-wasting in the long run than standing here arguing the toss.

As she fell in step beside Catrina as they walked to the study she wondered if the other girl was deranged or whether she simply enjoyed over-dramatising everything.

She didn't have time to ponder over Catrina's crazy-sounding words because as soon as they had gained the quiet, book-lined room the other girl closed the door, sank down gracefully on to a leather chesterfield and invited, 'Sit by me. I want to talk to you.'

'Just for a moment,' Imogen temporised. 'I've got such a lot to do.' Catrina was very striking, she thought as she did as she was told and sat down; with her mass of red-brown hair, creamy skin and strange green eyes she would never be able to hide in a crowd, and she wondered, fleetingly, why Alex had never been able to fall in love with her.

Pride that he had fallen in love with her, Imogen, instead, made her heart fill to bursting-point and there was a warm curve of a smile on her lips as she wondered what he was doing now. Probably looking for her...

And she was still smiling as Catrina said,

'You must know that Alex and I were engaged. Our parents wished it, for business reasons, you understand.'

'So I heard.' Imogen rearranged her face. A Cheshire-cat smile was not the most tactful expression to bring to a discussion about a broken engagement, even if it had been a completely amicable arrangement.

'Alex would have married me immediately, of course.' Catrina put her head on one side, a small, sly smile curving her mouth. 'You know how impetuous men can be. But I was very young at the time. There was so much I wanted to do and to see, I couldn't bear the thought of being tied down so soon. And eventually, with the help of my mother and his father, we got him to agree to a long engagement. I had every intention of marrying him, you know; he is very handsome and very rich, and one day our combined fortunes would have given us considerable clout—he might even have been persuaded to go into politics.'

Imogen shifted restlessly on her seat, trying not to look too impatient. It was true that she had a great deal to do and Catrina was wasting her time, but that was as nothing beside her distaste for the way Alex, her Alex, was being discussed.

She was about to say as much, and was searching for a tactful form of words, when Catrina pushed her hands through the riotous mass of her hair and stated dramatically, 'In the end, I just had to break it off. I know how much I hurt him, disappointed the parents, but I simply couldn't go through with it. Wild horses couldn't make me marry a man like that!'

Which wasn't the way Alex had told it, Imogen thought, almost feeling sorry for the girl. Doubtless it suited her image to have everyone believe that she was the one who had done the spurning, but she couldn't understand why Catrina was trying to convince *her*, who, as far as the other girl could know, was simply her ex-fiancé's colleague who happened to be acting as his hostess for this party.

And calling Alex a 'man like that' was more than a bit off, in her opinion. Gathering herself together, she gave Catrina a disapproving look.

'I really do have to go now. And I shouldn't worry if I were you; Alex will behave impeccably, I'm sure, and won't make you feel awkward over the broken engagement.' Indeed, Imogen recalled, having seen the two of them together earlier, she had been struck by the friendly atmosphere between them.

She got to her feet but Catrina's hands took hers in a surprisingly strong grip, forcing her back to the chesterfield again, and Imogen bit back a rush of angry protests, remembering just in time that, crazy or not, Catrina was a guest in this house.

But Catrina didn't sound crazy at all as she said, her voice low and sincere, 'Please listen; I'm not talking for the sake of it, I promise. It really does affect you.' Slowly, she released Imogen's hands and shook her head, biting down softly on her lower lip. 'It's not easy to say, because, in spite of everything, I still feel a certain loyalty to Alex.' She dragged in a shaky breath. 'But, having met you,

I can't just say nothing.' The green eyes suddenly looked misty. 'I mean, actually meeting someone is different from simply hearing about them, isn't it?'

Imogen stared back at her, a frown-line appearing between her huge violet eyes. What could Catrina have heard about her, and from whom? Tolly had probably mentioned her in the capacity as the head of the new agency venture, but surely that didn't merit this secret, dramatic discussion?

'I don't understand what you're getting at,' she stated, a shade impatiently, and Catrina smiled sympathetically.

'Of course you don't, why should you? Just let me explain.' She lolled back against the soft, grainy leather, her eyes half closed. 'When Alex and I first became engaged I was a little in awe of him, but later, as I grew older, more confident, I refused to be cowed. I told him that wearing his ring on my finger didn't give him automatic rights to my bed, and that didn't go down well with him, I can assure you.'

Imogen closed her eyes briefly against the searing stab of jealous pain then gritted her teeth.

Alex, as she knew, was a highly physical man and would not be slow to claim a fiancé's rights. That he had admitted that he had never been in love with Catrina wouldn't have made any difference. Men could have sex without their emotions being involved. They viewed such things differently, she had to remember that. And it would be strange if Alex had reached the age of thirty-six without having been involved in a sexual relationship.

'It was after that that I became aware of his ruthless streak. He can be charming, but he can be deadly, too. Oh, he didn't treat me shabbily; he knew how important financially our eventual marriage would be,' she confided, waving a slender hand dismissively through the air. 'But I began to see how he manipulated other people for his own ends—business associates and so on. I didn't like what I saw, and it was around then, I believe, that I made up my mind not to marry him. Some friends of mine have a home in the Bahamas, so I went there to think things over quietly and rationally.'

Imogen was hearing the second side of the same story but, on the whole, she believed Alex's version. She had to; she loved him, didn't she? And loving meant trusting. And it was just piqued vanity on Catrina's part that was making her so insistent on trying to prove that it was she, and not Alex, who had broken the engagement.

But what was said next turned that comforting idea on its head.

'I went back to New York, to my mother's home, fully determined to break off with Alex. I knew that a family Christmas had been planned and that Alex would be there. I told him what I'd decided and——' she shrugged prettily '—he was absolutely livid, as you can imagine. It was then, while he was so angry, he told me what he meant to do.' She allowed her heavy lids to drop over her eyes, as if sickened by what she was about to say, and Imogen felt her heart begin to pump against her ribs. She wanted to run from the room, away from what the other girl was saying, but her body remained just where it was as if incapable of obeying the dictates of her mind.

'He said,' Catrina whispered, '"If you're running out on me, then you won't much object if I get back to England to attend to some unfinished business. There's a clever little whore there who had her clutches into Tolly. I'm not going to be able to keep him over here, away from her, for much longer, so I'm going to make damn sure he sees the little slut for what she is. I'll get her into my bed, get her needing me like a drug. That should open the old fool's eyes. I'm not going to stand by and see him make the same mistake twice. I should have attended to it weeks ago, but couldn't actually bring myself to the point of doing anything about it. For one thing, second-hand goods don't appeal and, for another, strange as it must seem to you, I valued our relationship." At least, as far as I can recall, those were his very words, or as nearly so as makes no difference.'

'That's preposterous!' Imogen shot out, her colour rising. Alex loved her; he'd said so. He would never set out to do a thing like that.

She leapt to her feet. She wouldn't stay here and listen to one more word of this poison; but before she could reach the door Catrina was there, leaning back against the smooth, polished wood, her green eyes troubled.

'You're upset, of course you are,' she sympathised. 'But please think about what I've said. I only had to look at you to know that Alex has already become your lover. He's using you, and he'll turn you out of here, out of your job, too, the moment he's achieved his objective. Why do you think he gave you accommodation here? You'll be more easily ejected than if you were in the company flat.' She shook her head slowly from side to side. 'I don't know what your relationship with Tolly was, or what you hope it to be in the future, but I don't think you should be treated this way. And I'm not only thinking of you,' she went on emphatically when Imogen made a move to push past her, 'but of Tolly. Think of what it will do to him when Alex makes clear, as he will do, that you are his woman, share his bed. It's too cruel a way of showing Tolly that he's lost you for another, younger man. He's already looking strained and tired, or hadn't you noticed? I'd advise you to get out of here, tell Alex you're finished with him, before any more damage is done. You'd have to forfeit your new job, of course, but Alex intends to throw you out of it in any case, so wouldn't it be better to go now? Tolly has told us how talented you are, so getting another job shouldn't be much of a problem, should it?'

Later, Imogen never knew how she had walked away from Catrina, found her way to the kitchen. Everything was a blur, a senseless jumble, as she helped Mrs Hollins carry through the much-vaunted English tea which was to be served in the hall.

She couldn't believe a word Catrina had said. She wouldn't—never in a million years. She was simply a clever, scheming, spiteful cat!

Helping Mrs Hollins pass round the silver dish of hot, buttery muffins, she couldn't help notice how grey and drawn Tolly looked. Had the news of the broken engagement, the dynastic match he'd set his heart on, upset him so badly?

Catrina's stupid story, implying that he was worried because he believed his son had taken his mistress away from him, could be absolutely discounted because there wasn't, never had been, any truth in the rumour started by a silly gossip columnist who hadn't had anything better to do.

But she didn't have time to talk to her old friend; she was kept busy in her capacity as hostess, exchanging pleasantries with the Fishers, with Catrina's mother, who looked as if she had swallowed a lemon, sharing a joke with Pierre and agreeing with Stefan that rent-free accommodation in the excellent flat would be a so-good way to start saving to buy a small house to which he could bring his Eva when they were to be married.

A hand on the curve of her hip as she was pouring more hot water into the big silver teapot made her go rigid with tension. Alex. If she disbelieved all Catrina had said, then his touch shouldn't make all her muscles clench with rejection, should it?

Looking at him over her shoulder, she tried to relax, forced a smile, but there was a frown between his golden eyes as he looked down at her. He knew her so well.

'Where did you get to?' he queried softly. 'I couldn't find you.'

'Just talking to Catrina.' She knew she sounded stiff and unlike herself, but there was nothing she could do about it. She needed time on her own to think about the other girl's lies and finally banish them from her head, trashing them for the rubbish they were.

'You're all right?' His eyes probed hers and concern coloured his voice, and she nodded quickly.

'Just a headache, nothing much.' He couldn't be the devious bastard of Catrina's portrayal. Since he had returned on Christmas Eve he had shown her nothing but gentleness and love. Apart from their disagreement over where she would sleep, whether or not she should continue to share his bed after the guests arrived, a small, snide voice reminded, and she was still grappling with that when he said,

'I'll have to fetch Cathy now. Her train's due in ten minutes,' adding, for her ears alone, 'I'm already looking forward to the end of this shindig. I can't wait to have you to myself again.'

He walked away from her, making his excuses to his guests, and Imogen watched him, fighting back the awful premonition that she was watching him walk out of her life, that, after today, nothing could ever be the same again.

But that was utter nonsense, she told herself crossly, making herself smile and chatter as she re-filled teacups. A few minutes on her own would be enough to sort out all Catrina had said, satisfy herself that she had nothing to worry about.

Handing Tolly his second cup of tea, she gave him her warmest smile. Now that she had the first opportunity of the day to really look at him she could see what Catrina had meant. He looked drained and tired and a good ten years older than when she had last seen him, even wearier than she had initially thought.

'How are you?' she asked gently. 'I hope you haven't been overdoing things back in the States.'

He was a mere shadow of the man who had been so determined to acquire the London site for a brand new store, who had thrown himself whole-heartedly behind the agency venture. And he said, with a gallant attempt to recapture all his old light-heartedness, 'Not you, too! I've had enough ear-bending from that son of mine. Anyone would think there was a conspiracy among you young things to put me out to pasture!'

'If we worry about you, it's only because we're fond of you,' she replied softly, glad that the others had congregated around Catrina, who was holding forth on the delights of scuba-diving in the Bahamas.

It was the first opportunity she'd had to have a quiet talk with her old friend, to discover, if she could, if disappointment over Alex's broken engagement was the cause of his look of weary defeat. And he said quickly,

'I need to talk to you, Imogen. About your future, Alex, and a whole host of other things that seem to me to be very important.'

'Why not now?' she asked, her heart sinking. Had he too, as Catrina had claimed she had, picked up the vibes between Alex and herself, realised they were lovers? And, if so, was he blaming her for the break-up of the engagement he had been so happy about?

But Tolly lifted his shoulders in a wry shrug and murmured, 'I think it will have to be some other time, my dear,' as Tom Fisher detached himself from the group around Catrina and asked Tolly,

'Any chance you and I could get together with Alex and discuss setting up a meeting with the costing boys from the firm of builders you'll be using for the new store? There are a few things we need to get ironed out before we open negotiations.'

So that was that, and Imogen's annoyance wasn't entirely due to the lost opportunity to set Tolly's mind at rest about her part in the break-up between his son and Catrina. Alex had insisted that he had called the whole thing off before he and she had become lovers. She could remember vividly how relieved she'd been on hearing it. To anyone with eyes to see, Tolly was a tired man, in need of a few days' rest. He didn't need to have unlooked-for business meetings thrust upon him in the middle of what was supposed to be a couple of days of complete relaxation.

But it wasn't her place to say what was in her mind and she only hoped that Alex, when approached, would put the tin lid on the suggestion.

Mrs Hollins was collecting up the tea things, bristling with importance, determined to let the assembled guests know that, despite the hired staff who were making free with her kitchen, she was the one in charge around here.

Imogen went to help her but Alex came back right then with Cathy, her air of barely suppressed excitement, her bubbly personality making everyone smile.

'Isn't this just stupendous?' She greeted Imogen as if she were a long-lost friend. 'I just can't wait to start work on Monday morning; the new agency's the most exciting project I've ever been involved in!'

Introducing Cathy around, taking her to her room and settling her in, took longer than Imogen had imagined because the copywriter insisted on giving her a run-down on every last thing that had happened to her since they'd parted in Paris, ending up by demanding an opinion on the dress she had brought along to wear at that night's party.

'Do you think it's good enough?' She waved the slither of scarlet silk in front of Imogen's nose. 'The French are so sophisticated, aren't they? I don't want to look like an English country mouse!'

'Wearing that, you won't look like a mouse of any nationality,' Imogen grinned. She enjoyed the other girl's company and her light-hearted prattle went some way towards taking her mind off her own problems. 'But as there's only one French national here, am I to suppose——?'

'Suppose away! And you'd be right,' Cathy answered blithely, putting the wicked dress on a hanger, holding it out and staring at it with her head on one side. 'That last day in Paris, Pierre took me to lunch, went shopping with me, then we had dinner. Of course, he'd flirt with any female between eighteen and eighty—I know that—but he started something with me he's not going to be allowed to finish, although he doesn't know that yet!'

Feeling that the Gallic charmer had met his match at last, Imogen made her excuses and slipped away.

The corridor was quiet, no one about, and, away from Cathy's therapeutic chatter, she felt her head begin to ache again, as if there were a million warring thoughts in there, all battering around, looking for a way out.

Turning a corner, heading for the main staircase, she saw Alex come out of the room they shared and her heart gave the familiar leap. He was so dear to her, so very much loved. She couldn't let herself believe the things Catrina had said.

'I've been looking for you.' He took a step towards her, enfolding her gently in his arms. 'I miss you when you're not right where I can see you.'

Briefly, she allowed herself the exquisitely comforting solace of resting her aching head against the breadth of his sweater-clad chest, breathing in the clean male scent of him, absorbing the beat of his heart into her own. She needed him so, needed him to tell her that Catrina was a congenital liar, that no one, but no one, could ever believe a word she said.

But what Catrina had said was something she was going to have to try to understand, all by herself, and suddenly a wave of nausea attacked her, and she jerked back in his arms, clenching her teeth.

'You look done-in, pet,' he said caressingly and she closed her ears to the rich seduction of his beautiful voice and protested,

'I'm all right,' wishing he'd go because she couldn't think straight when he was around.

'You don't look it.' His hands were gently kneading her shoulders, finding the tense muscles at the back of her neck, and his touch, far from relaxing her, knotted her up completely, and he looked down into her pale face and instructed, 'Rest on the bed for a couple of hours. I've checked with the staff from the caterers and everything's in hand downstairs. Most of the guests are relaxing, either in their rooms or round the sitting-room fire, and Tolly, Fisher and I are about to have an informal policy-meeting in the study.'

That statement cleared her mind a little, prompted her to say, her voice tarter than she'd meant it to be, 'I thought you might have scotched that idea—Tolly looks so tired. He could do with a good long rest, not yet another business meeting. You should take better care of him!'

She felt his withdrawal, the way his body tensed, his hands dropping from her shoulders, and his voice had fallen several degrees in temperature as he riposted, 'Anyone would think you had a vested interest in my father's state of health. But don't worry—I take as much care of him as he will allow me to. And the only reason I agreed to Fisher's suggestion of an informal meeting was to twist Tolly's arm into agreeing to let the dog get a look at the rabbit. We do have an adequate company set-up, which is going into gear right now, to handle the way we establish new stores. He doesn't have to do every damn thing himself.'

He walked away, his voice coming curtly in the heavy silence that wrapped the upper part of the house, 'I know what I'm doing; just pay me the compliment of letting me get on with it in my own way, will you?'

Imogen felt sick with tension as she let herself into the room she had so blissfully shared with Alex, the past tense being the operative factor, she thought on a note of anguish as, her stomach churning violently, she flicked on the overhead light and raced for the adjoining bathroom, only just making it in time before she was wretchedly sick.

Creeping back into the bedroom and on to the bed, flicking off the light because it hurt her eyes, she acknowledged miserably that her body was giving her messages about the facts her mind had been fighting to ignore.

His 'Anyone would think you had a vested interest in my father's state of health' had brought them back to square one, hadn't it?

She could no longer ignore what Catrina had said, write it off as a pack of malicious lies.

Lying in the darkness, the silence, she made herself acknowledge the facts. Alex had said he loved her, but words cost nothing, and he'd made it very plain he had no intention of marrying her. And, when she'd tried to explain the innocence of her relationship with Tolly, he'd brushed her attempts aside with an offhanded, 'Sure. I gave you a bad time, but it's all forgotten now.'

But it hadn't been forgotten—none of it—and she'd been a fool not to state her case more clearly, insist that he listen to every word she said.

He'd used her, as Catrina had pointed out. Abused her. Got her into his bed with the sole intention of rescuing his father from her supposedly greedy clutches. No wonder he'd been so annoyed when she'd suggested that their openly sharing a room wouldn't be very tactful, in view of his recently broken engagement, when Catrina, her mother and Tolly were among the guests!

When he had first begun to display a sexual interest in her she had been quick to ferret out the reasons behind his sudden turn-around. Threats, offers to buy her off hadn't worked, so he'd tried to demonstrate to his father that she could be anybody's, provided the price was right.

So she'd been aware of his motives all along and, fool that she was, she had pushed them right out of her mind, blinded by her stupid love for him.

She turned restlessly on the bed, burying her head in the pillow, refusing to cry because tears wouldn't alter anything. But the pillow carried the evocative scent of his expensive aftershave and she squirmed herself into a sitting position, clasping her arms around her knees.

Regrets were futile. She had to think of the future. Alex was intending to throw her out of his bed, out of his house and out of her job. But she had been forewarned and she supposed she should be thanking Catrina for that. Her head had been calling the other girl a liar, half crazy, but her heart had known better all along.

There was no way Catrina could have known about her supposed affair with Tolly, Alex's violent objection to the very idea of it, the way he had pushed her into a corner over the matter of accommodation, handing over the flat she'd been promised to the two men. No way she could have known unless Alex himself had told her.

And that was the final, damning proof. All she needed to recognise.

CHAPTER ELEVEN

'I'LL drop you off at the station, if you like,' Cathy said, fastening her trench-coat. 'I'll just pop through and say goodnight to the boys.' One eye closed in a mischievous wink and Imogen made herself smile and reply,

'Thanks, it will save me ringing through for a taxi,' and watched the other girl swing out of the office, heading for the layout-room.

The first day for the agency had gone smoothly, even though they'd been hectically busy. Keeping her nose firmly to the grindstone had been a life-saver, she thought as she began to tidy her desk. Stopped her from wondering when Alex would walk through the door.

But he hadn't put in an appearance and she pushed her typed letter of resignation back into a drawer. The moment he'd showed his face she would have given it to him, but since he hadn't turned up she supposed she would have to post it.

Three months was the length of time stipulated in her contract and, although she would have preferred it to be much less, it did at least give her time to find new employment. She wasn't hanging around for him to give her the push!

It had been surprisingly easy to walk out of Kynaston seventy-two hours ago. Using the phone at the side of the bed, she had contacted one of her girlfriends, a former colleague at Martin and Sandown's, begging for a bed for the night. Jenny's East End flat was tiny but she'd said,

'I can offer a sofa. It's yours for as long as you want it—lumps and all,' and although she'd obviously been intrigued she hadn't asked questions, which was just as well because Imogen had got herself straightened out, back to the basics that told her that she'd always been right, been most contented when she'd refused to admit emotional relationships into her life.

And if her three colleagues at the agency wondered why she had disappeared from Kynaston on the night of the house-warming party, had opted to travel daily from London, they had kept their queries to themselves.

Another phone call had booked a taxi to take her and a hastily packed bag to Jenny's, and all that had remained was to write a note, secure it to the pillow where Alex would find it, and get herself outside.

Fortunately, there'd been no one around to witness her silent departure and she'd walked down the drive to meet the taxi, resolutely pushing Alex, and the way he had used her, out of her mind.

The note she had scrawled had been the last emotional outburst she would ever allow herself. The bitter words had been the product of the final spasm of hurt.

Fun while it lasted, but I'm moving out. Other fish to fry. You're the one with the tricky mind, so I'll leave you to work out what to tell your guests.

She had shut him out of her heart and whether she ever saw him again or whether she did not was inconsequential because he couldn't touch her emotions ever again.

So why, when the phone rang on her desk, and she picked it up and heard his voice say her name, did her heart twist cruelly, making her breath clog in her lungs?

'Speaking,' she clipped out as soon as she'd hauled herself together, reminding herself that she didn't hate him because hatred was an emotion, wasn't it, and she was never allowing any of those disruptive forces into her life again?

'I'm picking you up in two minutes flat.'

The words were iced over, brooking no argument, but she argued, anyway, 'Don't waste your time. I won't be here. I've already left, as far as you're concerned.'

He said, 'Bitch!' very quietly, his hatred of her coming through intensely in spite of that. 'Tolly was taken into hospital early this morning. Heart attack. I've been with him all day. He's asking to see you; God knows why. But if he wants you, he's going to get you. I'm up at the house,' he ended tersely. 'Be ready to leave in two minutes.'

Imogen was in shock as she replaced the receiver, her eyes unfocused as Cathy breezed back into the room, having to shake herself into some semblance of normality as the other girl said, 'Ready when you are.'

'You go ahead.' Her tongue felt thick in her mouth; she could hardly get her words out. 'I'll be catching a later train. See you in the morning.' She couldn't bring herself to explain what had happened—she could hardly take it in herself and, left to herself, she dragged on her coat, fastening it with shaky fingers, trying to tell herself that Tolly would be all right.

Dear God, don't let him die, she prayed silently and fervently, and hoped with awful desperation that fretting over the broken engagement between his son and Catrina hadn't brought the attack on, that he hadn't believed her responsible for the rift.

Heaven knew, it wasn't true, but he had no way of knowing of Alex's paranoid suspicions, his dreadful plan to discredit her. He had said he wanted to talk to her, about Alex, about her future, and she'd thought at the time that he'd had the broken engagement in mind. She couldn't live with that kind of guilt if anything happened to Tolly, even though she knew the guilt would be misplaced.

And who had been kidding who when she'd told herself that her emotions were dead? she derided herself as Alex arrived, his face set, fatigue staring dully out of his eyes. He still had the power to move her, to make her yearn to be able to cradle his dark head between her hands, to kiss the lines of concern away from around his eyes, his mouth, to assure him that Tolly would be fine.

But who was she to assure him of anything? And she was the last person whose sympathy he needed.

'How is he?' she asked quickly as the Jaguar pulled away down the drive, risking a glance at his rock-hard profile, wondering at his power to still hurt her. The emotions he'd brought to life after long years of atrophy simply wouldn't lie down and die again, and the pain in her heart had as much to do with her own hurt as with poor Tolly's plight.

'Ill,' he said grimly. Then, his mouth tightening, 'Don't tell me you really care? I didn't think you capable of caring about anything except your own selfish interests.'

Coming from him, that was just too much, and the surge of boiling anger that had her on the edge of her seat, twisting her hands together to stop the impulse to hit him, was the final proof that she could no longer order her emotions. They had taken over before, because of him, and looked like continuing in the same foolhardy fashion.

If she spoke to him at all it would all come pouring out, all the hatred, bitterness and pain. Such humiliation she could do without, so she bit her tongue and said nothing as the car raced through the winter streets, breaking speed regulations in a way that once would have had her jittery with nerves.

But he went on bitingly, as if determined to inflict all the punishment he could, 'He was already overtired, and your walking out on me on the night of the party didn't help. Believe it or not, the relationship you and I had mattered to him. Fortunately, he had no way of knowing what was in that love-letter you left me, otherwise he'd have really gone under.' The icy sarcasm in his voice wasn't lost on Imogen and she cringed under the sting of it.

At the time it had been her only means of lashing out, a cruelty inflicted for cruelty received, and his remark about her relationship with Alex mattering to Tolly didn't make any sense, and she didn't have time to puzzle it out because she was still cringing when he ground out, 'Fortunately, he's a survivor, and he's had an unpleasant demonstration of what overwork, at his age, can do to a man. And that's a statement of fact, not an attempt to ease your guilt.'

He had slowed down now, entering the hospital environs, and she shot him a seething look and threw out, 'You can't make me feel guilty over what happened to Tolly, so don't try!'

He jerked the brakes on, staring straight ahead at the lighted windows of the intensive-care unit, and told her tonelessly, 'I'm not. Not even I can get blood out of a stone. You didn't give a tinker's damn when you walked out on me, and when you've finished frying your other poor fish you'll walk out on him without a backward glance.'

His fingers drummed restlessly against the wheel, but otherwise he could have been carved out of stone, and Imogen swallowed painfully because she knew she deserved that nasty gibe. Implying she'd left him for another lover was the only way she'd been able to inflict a little pain in retaliation for the much larger agony he'd inflicted on her.

But it was backfiring on her and it was difficult to cope with the disgust in his voice as he grated, 'All that guff about being put off marriage by your parents' life together was just a blind, wasn't it? The truth is that you're incapable of staying faithful to one man for more than a week or two.'

Seething, Imogen released her seatbelt and scrambled out of the car, her mouth set as she reminded him, 'We're wasting time. Just show me where Tolly is and get lost!'

Even if that last insulting gibe were true, it couldn't matter to him. His only interest had been in demonstrating to Tolly just what a tramp she was! But she wasn't here to trade insults with him. If she started to point out the several and various facets of his own nasty nature she would be here forever!

'Just a few moments, no more,' someone in a white overall warned her, opening the door to the private room where Tolly lay on a stark, high bed, connected to bits of equipment that made Imogen go cold just to look at them.

Finding herself alone with the sick man, she couldn't have said if the person who had admitted her had been male or female, and she took a careful, calming breath before approaching the bed. Tolly's eyes opened heavily.

'Thank you for coming.'

'Don't talk,' she instructed gently, heeding the warning given her earlier, though how she was to get to know why he had asked to see her, if he wasn't allowed to speak, she didn't know.

But that was not important, she affirmed as she pulled up a chair and took the hand he held out to her, closing her fingers around it as it lay on the counterpane. 'I'll come to see you every day,' she promised. 'You just rest and get your strength back.'

'No good,' he frowned impatiently. 'Don't pussyfoot around. Just tell me why you walked out on my boy.' He broke off, struggling for breath, and she looked around wildly for a bell to summon the medical staff but he said, with a trace of his old vigour, 'Look me in the eye and tell me what went wrong, damn it! I want to know.'

'I don't think we should talk about it right now,' Imogen said worriedly. 'You shouldn't get yourself in a state; it's the worst thing for you.'

'Lying here worrying is going to get me in a worse state,' he said with undeniable logic. 'It wasn't a serious attack, and I'll be free of these contraptions by tomorrow. So what went wrong? Alex loves you. You can't just walk away from him. I know he can be pretty high-handed at times so, if you've had a spat, why can't you talk it out? And maybe I'm old-fashioned, but you should marry him. He told me why you were anti it but I want my grand-children legitimate.'

This was worse, far worse, than she had ever thought possible. Tolly was obviously rambling; perhaps he thought he was talking to Catrina! And she said, as warmly and gently as her misery would allow, 'Don't worry about it now. Alex doesn't feel anything for me; he was just pretending.' No point in upsetting him further and explaining how that pretence had come about! 'He wouldn't want to marry me if I came wrapped up in a million dollars.'

'Don't humour me, woman!' Tolly achieved as near a roar as his shortage of breath allowed. 'Do you think I'd believe my own son capable of lying to me? He came over to the States just to get everything straight with me. Told me he'd started out believing you were after me—for my money, mind, insulting wretch!—and ended up falling for you. Broke his engagement with Catrina, of course, and I put him right about our relationship. Although, as he said at the time, it didn't matter a toss, because even if I did want you I wasn't going to get you. You were his! Then he hightailed it back to London, to be with you, with my blessing, if anyone's interested. He'd told me how he'd managed to get you securely under his roof, and the rest, as he said, was a matter of chemistry. Though he did say he was going to have to work on getting you to marry him. It was that I wanted to talk to you about on the night of the party you ran out on. And don't look at me like that!'

His grumbled remark told her he'd noticed the way her mouth had fallen open, and stayed open. She closed it quickly, aware that, suddenly, she was shaking all over, wanting to cry. And she managed thickly, 'Who told Catrina all this?' because one thing was sure—Alex hadn't, or at least not the way his ex-fiancé had told it.

'I did.' Tolly stared at her, his eyebrows bristling, looking a thousand per cent more alert than he had done ten minutes ago. 'We flew over together, with 'Stasia, didn't we? 'Stasia was a bit put out by the news that the engagement was off. Didn't bother me, though; I'd never seen Alex look happier than when he'd told me he loved you. And his happiness is all I care about. And Catrina took it like a trooper, even told us she'd been having second thoughts herself on account of some man she met in the Bahamas. So, to enliven an otherwise tedious journey, I told the pair of them about Alex thinking you were trying to lead me up the aisle, the lengths he had gone to to get you precisely where he wanted you. Thought it mildly hilarious myself—so did Catrina.'

No, she didn't, Imogen corrected inside her head. Catrina didn't find the situation amusing at all; she simply hid her reactions well. She'd set out with deliberate intent to ruin her affair with Alex, taking the facts as Tolly had related them, giving them a twist here and there and attributing them to Alex!

She could feel herself shaking inside, her emotions running riot as she stared, wide-eyed, at the man on the bed. How could she have believed Catrina? How could she have been such a fool?

And Tolly said gruffly, 'You and he were meant for each other. I saw it that night you both had dinner with me at my hotel. We were celebrating the acquisition of the site for the new store and I remember thinking that he was out to get you, and you wouldn't know what had hit you, and the next celebration would come at your wedding. So cut along,' he smiled at her tiredly. 'Put right what's gone wrong between you—and don't let it happen again.'

'I will,' Imogen promised, and got to her feet. Her knees shook under her but she managed to smile as she bent to put a light kiss on his forehead. 'And you take care now; we can't do with any more shocks in the family.'

The family, she thought shakily, as she closed his door behind her. It sounded good. So very good. She'd never had a proper family life—her parents' fights had seen to that—and she had never known, until now, just how much she'd missed it.

And, loving her, Alex had wanted to marry her, and together they would have created a warm, close-knit family of their own, with Tolly caring more for her than her own father had ever done.

But she had blown it!

Briefly, she leaned against the wall of the corridor, closing her eyes. The love Alex had felt for her had probably been killed, turned to hatred, by the way she had left him, the things she had said. She didn't know, but she was going to have to find out.

She pulled herself upright as one of the medical staff walked into Tolly's room, giving her a curious look. She was shivering, despite her warm, holly-red wool coat, and she didn't know whether Alex had waited for her or whether he'd done as she'd told him and 'got lost'.

Her legs unsteady, she walked down the corridor to the waiting-room and her heart lurched with love and fear as she saw Alex on one of the metal-framed chairs. He was slumped, his dark head bent, his eyes on the floor and, for a moment, she stood watching him, afraid to approach him because he might just tell her he never wanted to lay eyes on her again.

But he looked up, as if sensing her presence, and she could have wept for the strain, the weariness in his eyes. And then they hardened, shutting her out, and he asked tightly, 'How is he now?'

She shrugged slightly, her eyes miserable. 'I can't judge, but he seemed brighter, stronger, when I left him. Are you going to see him?'

If he was, she would wait. She would wait forever for the opportunity to put things right between them. But once love had gone, had been killed by lack of trust, by sheer cruelty, could it ever come to life again?

'Not tonight.' He was on his feet, reaching for the sheepskin he'd left on one of the other chairs. 'Rest will do him more good. I'll run you to the station.'

Just like that. He didn't want to know. Didn't want her around. She was going to have to convince him that he did. Somehow.

She had never felt more nervous in her life and she pushed her tongue over dry, tremulous lips and said thickly, 'Can we talk? There's something I think you should know.'

He'd been walking ahead of her to the door and he hadn't heard her mumbled words because he turned, his black brows drawn together impatiently. 'Sorry? Did you say something?'

So Imogen had to repeat her request and that increased her nervousness a thousand-fold, and she felt even worse when he asked tautly, 'What should I know? I've had a long, traumatic day and I'm not in the mood for female dissembling, and I can't think you could tell me anything I would want to know.'

'I love you,' she stated, distraught. In the face of his implacable dislike it had taken a lot of courage to get that out and she wasn't going to back down now, retreat—not even when he gave her a long, hard stare, one brow rising cynically as he bit out,

'Your brand of love I can do without. I'd feel easier with any other woman's bitter enmity! What's wrong? Doesn't your new lover come up to scratch in bed?' He walked out, leaving her to follow, and she had to run to keep up with his long, angry stride, her high heels making a frantic pattern of sound in the quiet corridor. And she caught at his arm as he strode across the car park at a pace that made her breathless, and she was red in the face, her temper rising.

She told him indignantly, 'I know what you think, and why you think it. But you're wrong. And I could tell you why, if you'd damn well listen!'

His pace, if anything, increased, but she held doggedly on, her heart racing with fear because she didn't know how to make him stand still long enough to hear what she was trying to say. Finally she yelled frustratedly, 'It all started with you thinking I was after Tolly, and ended with a load of lies Catrina told me!'

He stopped then, but only because they'd reached his car, and he turned slowly, his face ghastly in the harsh, overhead lights.

'What lies? What did Catrina tell you?'

And this was her chance, the only one she would get, and she told him all his ex-fiancée had said, ignoring the bitter, rain-laden wind, and she ended wistfully, wondering if her words had made any difference, not thinking they had, because his features were tight, not giving anything away.

'At the time it all seemed to make sense. It added up. But something Tolly said just now made me realise I'd been wrong.'

' "Something Tolly said",' Alex repeated on a note of bitterness that filled her with a numbing sense of hopelessness. 'It wouldn't have occurred to you to ask my opinion?'

'You didn't hear the way Catrina told it,' she muttered miserably in her own defence, and Alex unlocked the car door, instructing tersely,

'Get in.'

She did, misery swamping her. He had heard all she had to say and it had made no difference. Lack of trust on her part had ruined everything. And, as he started the engine, she asked, her defeat evident in the weary note of her voice, 'Where are we going?' If he said, 'to the station', she would put back her head and howl, she knew she would, because he would be letting her know she didn't stand a chance, she had had her say and it had made no difference.

But he said, expressionlessly, 'Home,' and her heart leapt wildly, just for a second, before she warned herself not to count any chickens.

In the mood he was in he was probably taking her back to Kynaston to pack the clothes she hadn't been able to take with her on the night of the party. And then he would take her and her gear to the station. Or, more likely, phone for a taxi. He wouldn't want any trace of her left in his home.

Nothing was said on the journey back. She thought it best to leave him to his brooding silence, and she couldn't think of anything to say, in any case. She had said it all, and it hadn't been enough.

And her back was rigid with tension as she walked in front of him to the sitting-room, and she had to blink back tears as she watched him kneel before the banked-up fire and stir it into flaring life.

The room was warm, the central-heating system excellent, but then, only the best would do for Alexsander Devenko. And that would go for the women he admitted into his life, she acknowledged defeatedly. So that ruled her out. She was flawed, had behaved in an outrageously over-emotional way—running out on him, on an important celebration. Her action would have made him look a fool, or worse.

Trouble was, once her emotions had been brought back to life they'd become unruly, impossible to handle, pushing her ability to think coolly and logically out of sight.

'Your coat?' The upward twist of one black brow was the only expression on Alex's stony face. He had removed his own coat, and the black fine-knit sweater and narrow trousers he wore made him look utterly menacing.

Fighting the stupid impulse to give in to his domination, Imogen clipped coolly, 'I'm not staying.' He had only brought her here to collect the remainder of her gear, she was quite sure about that, and she wasn't going to be browbeaten into meek compliance to his every dictate. She did have some pride left.

And something angry looked out of his eyes as they sparked into brilliant golden life, and a muscle jerked at the corner of his jaw as, with a few deft, economical movements, he divested her of the red wool coat.

'You're not running out on me again,' he imparted grimly, tossing the garment to join his sheepskin which lay in a heap on an elegant brocade-covered chaise longue. 'You said you loved me,' he bit out, his eyes glittering dangerously. 'What kind of love so easily believes the very worst? I don't think it's the kind I want anything to do with.'

He could denigrate everything else, but not the love she felt for him; it was too precious to allow him to drag it through the mire. And she felt her temper rise, and that, even if she had needed proof, told her that as far as this one man was concerned her emotions would always have the upper hand. She hadn't meant this encounter to develop into a slanging match but it was out of her hands and she snapped right back.

'And what about yours? You said you'd been falling in love with me, almost from the moment we met, yet you still thought I was a cheap tramp. You had to have Tolly's confirmation of the opposite before you allowed yourself to sully your hands with me!'

She had no idea if she was making sense, and didn't care, but her rage abated to a silent simmer as she watched comprehension, followed by shock, cross his beloved features. But he didn't say anything, not then, turning on his heel after giving her one long, puzzled look. And she heard the tiny clatter as the neck of a decanter met glass and when she turned he silently held out a brandy to her and poured himself another.

'You are absolutely, devastatingly right,' he told her, lifting his glass in an unspoken salute, and there was a thread of emotion she couldn't put a name to in his voice but which effectively washed away the very last trace of anger. 'I was only seeing things from my own point of view,' he admitted, swallowing the brandy in one irreverent gulp and, watching the strong line of his throat, the firm ripple of muscles, Imogen felt her mouth go dry, the familiar longing for him burning her up.

He put his glass down and exhaled sharply, his eyes frowning. 'God knows, I was quick enough to believe the worst of you, even though I knew I was beginning to want you as I'd never wanted another woman. I was jealous of my own father, didn't know which way to turn. I knew I only had to touch you to have you turn into flame, but I kept holding back, telling myself you were on the make, would turn on for any man if the price was right. But if any other man so much as smiled at you I nearly went wild.' His mouth twisted wryly. 'I was fast becoming a suitable case for treatment.'

He took several quick, tense paces across the room, stopped in front of the fire, staring into it for long, silent moments before turning, his eyes boring into hers.

'Do you love me enough to forgive me for that?'

She nodded, her heart too full to allow speech. She would forgive Alex anything, always, as long as he loved her, and she was beginning to know he did.

'Come here.' His arms were open to her and she went to them, laying her head against the breadth of his chest, but he caught her chin in one hand, tilting her head, making her meet his eyes. Which was no hardship at all, she thought muzzily, seeing the love in the beautiful amber depths.

'There are certain things you have a right to know,' he began, his deep voice thrilling her as always. But she didn't want him to talk, not now, and she put a finger over his lips, her own parting with helpless invitation.

And he smiled, as if he knew exactly what she was feeling, as he always would, his eyes glinting wickedly as he took her fingertips between his white teeth, gently nipping, before shaking his head. 'Correction. There are things I need you to know. I don't want you to go on thinking that I normally think the worst of everyone and refuse to listen to their side of the story!' Both hands cupped her face, his thumbs softly stroking her cheekbones. 'When I read that piece about you and Tolly I panicked. And that's not something I do all the time, believe me.'

Imogen believed him. He was one of the strongest characters she knew and, if he wanted to talk, then talk he would, and if she didn't interrupt him he would get it all out of his system and they could revisit, together, that wonderful place where words weren't needed at all.

'I'd seen it happen to Tolly before,' he went on calmly. 'My mother died when I was nine; he and

I were both shattered. She was a dearly loved lady. Then, six years later, he remarried. Janice was very lovely and about half his age and even I, at the age of fifteen, could see what she was after. But Tolly was blind where she was concerned, and lonely, needing love and marriage, flattered because such a beautiful young thing should return his love. She didn't, of course. The only thing Janice loved about Tolly was his money. She spent the three years she was with him spending the stuff as if it were going out of fashion, partying, sleeping around.'

Despite her policy of non-interruption, Imogen couldn't help the small cry of outrage. How could anyone treat poor Tolly that way?

And Alex said grimly, 'There's worse. He was still blinded by her physical attributes, couldn't see the ugly, greedy soul for the brilliant packaging, and she made him look a fool. By that time everyone knew exactly what she was, were sniggering at him behind their hands.' His voice roughened. 'I couldn't stand to see him being made a laughing-stock; he's a fine man. And when the show-down came, it was all my doing. I told him exactly what she was up to, pointed out that he was a blind old idiot, refusing to see what was staring him in the face. Not very tactful, but then I was eighteen years old, not strong on that particular commodity.

'He was getting ready for yet another party that was to be held in our home,' he recalled grimly, his eyes in the past. 'And I'd gone to his room. I knew that a certain muscle-bound third-rate film actor was to be there, the latest in the endless line of my stepmother's conquests, and I could no longer hold back on what I knew, what everyone knew. So I let him have it. And, for the first time in my life, Tolly hit me. I was already taller and broader than he, but I was still reeling from the emotional shock when I joined the party an hour or so later. I usually kept well away from them. It made me sick to see the way she acted, the way people sniggered, the way Tolly was so damned blind! And, as I'd known, Janice was giving the actor guy the heavy come-on, and he was in no way objecting.

'At first, I tried to be adult about it, went up to them and asked him to leave—rather politely, I thought at the time—and told Janice I'd prefer it if she didn't embark on affairs right in front of my father and his guests. And this film guy—I can't even remember the bastard's name—said, "Jealous, kid? Why not try being patient? All things come to he who waits—and that includes your stepmother—when you've grown up a bit!"'

'And then all hell broke loose. I'm not proud of it, but I lit into him like a maniac and it took three other guys to drag me off him. Tolly divorced her shortly after and for a year he was a broken man. I watched him fall apart. And it was several years before he was really back to his old self again.'

'And you helped him,' Imogen put in, appalled by the dreadful glimpse into her old friend's past, and Alex nodded soberly.

'I hope so. And when he really started to take an interest again, in life, in the business, and came up with the suggestion that Catrina and I could do a lot worse than marry each other, I agreed. At least in principle. Catrina was very young and seemed to think that being engaged would be fun, and if, as I had stipulated, there was to be no talk of an actual marriage for at least five years, then there was always the very real chance that she would find someone to fall in love with. Our engagement,' he said drily, 'was a highly impersonal affair.'

Which wasn't the way Catrina had told it, but Imogen didn't believe a word of what the other woman had said, and she snuggled more closely into the haven of Alex's arms and whispered, 'Thank you for telling me this. You needn't have done.'

'There was every need,' he told her huskily, his mouth against the pulse-point at her temple. 'It will help you to understand why I went into a panic when I thought what had happened to Tolly before was about to happen all over again.'

'Yet you never properly apologised,' she said, lifting her face, her lips trailing over his jawline, belying the mock severity of her voice. 'Not even when you'd heard from the horse's mouth that I wasn't out to tie your father up in matrimonial knots.'

'I'd meant to,' he confessed, sounding, for the first time ever, unsure of himself. 'But when I arrived back here, the night before Christmas, meaning to ask your forgiveness, you were so warm, so beautiful. All I could think of was claiming you for myself. You did start to say something about the innocence of your relationship with Tolly, and I was too much of a coward to take it any further. I thought if I told you everything, reminded you of just how badly I'd thought of you—bracketing you with that bitch Janice—you would, quite rightly, blow your top and give me my marching orders!'

With a low groan of protest that denied she would ever do such a thing, Imogen reached up and twined her arms around his neck, meeting his mouth hungrily, and she felt his heartbeats quicken, thudding against her breasts, and when she broke away, breathless, on fire with need, he murmured throatily, 'Tell me you love me. Say you'll never leave me.'

So she did, over and over, between wild, eager kisses, and as he scooped her up into his arms she clung to him weakly, knowing where he was taking her, mentally making over the rest of her life to him.

And he said thickly, 'I love you more than life,' and that was all she needed to hear, with one single exception, and she put her mouth against his, whispering against his skin,

'You never did ask me to marry you,' and he chuckled, his arms tightening around her as he walked through the door, heading for the stairs.

'Only because I knew you were so anti. I was working up to it.'

And she smiled softly into his eyes, loving him, always loving him.

'Then you can take a break. You just convinced me.'

HARLEQUIN®

PRESENTS Plus

Meet Samantha Maxwell, a sensitive, naive and incredibly innocent woman, and Matthew Putnam, a man who's as rich as sin and about to ruin Samantha's life.

And then there's Andrea Markham, a concert pianist who's desperately attracted to her manager. But to what end—Luke Kane is a bachelor at heart!

These are just some of the passionate men and women you'll discover each month in Harlequin Presents Plus—two longer and dramatic new romances by some of the best-loved authors writing for Harlequin Presents. Share their exciting stories—their heartaches and triumphs—as each falls in love.

Don't miss
RICH AS SIN by Anne Mather,
Harlequin Presents Plus #1567
and
BACHELOR AT HEART by Roberta Leigh,
Harlequin Presents Plus #1568

Harlequin Presents Plus
The best has just gotten better!

Available in July wherever Harlequin books are sold.

PPLUS2